THE GREAT HYDRATION

Fiction by Barrington Bayley

THE GREAT HYDRATION

Barrington Bayley

COSMOS BOOKS

THE GREAT HYDRATION

Cosmos Books, an imprint of Wildside Press
PO Box 301, Holicong, PA 18928-0301
www.wildsidepress.com

For more information, contact Wildside Press.

ISBN: 1-58715-510-9

CHAPTER ONE

The desert rover laboured up the slope, sand falling from its long wheelspokes, until it gained the top of the big dune. There the driver disengaged the inner and outer wheels and jerked a lever which applied the brake. The vehicle came to an abrupt halt, its inner wheels continuing ineffectually to turn, still driven by the never-ceasing radium motor.

The two Analane who had come so far gazed fascinated down the other side of the dune. A range of distant hills marked the limit of a level plain. In the foreground stood the numerous pavilions of the World Market, their bright colours glittering against the shining yellow sand.

"Our journey is over. We have arrived."

Hrityu, the driver, turned to glance at his companion Kurwer. Both were typical of the tribe of the Analane: humanoid, lean, rubbery, skin a luminous blue in colour, purple crests dividing their smooth pates. Hrityu raised an arm as slender as the rest of him, and began to name the various pavilions which were scattered over two langs or more. In the midst of the complex was the huge Hydrorium, the refuge of the market masters, fronted by the gaudy Pavilion of Audience where they deigned to meet with visitors. Round about lay the Pavilion of Mining, the Pavilion of Vehicles, the Pavilion of Extravagances, and more—all places where bargains could be struck, and knowledge and techniques exchanged between races from anywhere across the globe.

"And there is the one we want, Kurwer. The Pavilion of Warfare." Hrityu veered his finger towards a structure that, unlike the brilliant hues of the other buildings, was made of a dull grey metal.

"Let us hope we shall get what we want," Kurwer murmured, overawed by the sight.

"With what we have to offer, we should do a good deal."

He engaged the rover's inner and outer wheels once more, releasing the brakes. They braced themselves as the machine lurched slithering down the dune's collapsing slope. Soon they were on level ground and rolling towards the brilliant shapes ahead.

Hrityu steered towards the concourse that ran through the middle of the market. Kurwer, who was on his first visit, gawped as the pavilions rose around them, and stared at the creatures of many tribes and races that they passed. Hrityu made immediately for the vehicle park, drove into it, found a space and stopped.

They climbed out, and became aware of a chorus of soft humming noises. It came from the radium motors of the vehicles parked around them, which could not be switched off once they were assembled and to which the voice of their own vehicle's motor was added.

The park itself was indeed a wonderland, littered with carriages of various kinds from all over the planet. There were cars mounted on big rollers filled with air. There were walking carriages. There were vehicles running on treads and tracks, and leaping parachute vehicles which could traverse lava swamps by kicking themselves into the air and guiding themselves onto a firm spot from which to kick off again. There were crawling vehicles which flipped or screwed themselves through the sand, and boat-like, sharp-keeled vehicles which coursed hissing over the desert propelled by blasts of air.

But at the entrance to the park was a curious sculpture of great antiquity, much corroded by sand abrasion. It resembled slightly one of the air-jet sandboats, but its sides were taller. Vertical poles sprang from its superstructure, one of them broken short, and from these sprang fragments of what once had been billowing sheet-like shapes.

The two Analane but glanced at it as they left the park. No one in the present-day world built such a craft, nor was there any need to.

Instead they devoted their attention to the sights and scenes around them, for this was the one cosmopolitan spot upon the entire surface of the world. Most of those thronging the concourse were humanoid. There were giant Yongs, nearly twice the height of an Analane and a pale yellow in colour, with bright, slitted eyes. There were squat Grishis, whose orange-coloured bodies made them look like lumps of sandstone. There were Jodobrocks, Limes, and even a few coal-black Gamintes with red eyes and wiry, sparkling, silver hair.

Also there were nonhumanoids of the sand-burrowing lizard family, distinguishable from one another by size and the patterns of colour on their corrugated hides, walking sinuously on their hind limbs and trailing thick tails which left wavy tracks in the sand. Hrityu even glimpsed a lone Sawune with its white, soft-looking skin, whose kind dug deep under the desert where it was very cold. The Sawune was clad in a long loose garment to ward off the day's heat. Nearly blind, it wore shades over its eyes as protection from the sunlight.

So many passed to and fro that they kicked up a continuous mist of fine sand. Kurwer cleared it from his membranes with a rasping, coughing noise.

"This is like being in a sandstorm."

"You'll have to get used to it," Hrityu told him, wheezing a little himself. "It's always like this."

"Well, let's get inside as quickly as possible!" Kurwer looked about him at the accommodation houses that were interspersed between the pavilions. "Which lodging shall we go to?"

Suddenly he stiffened. His hand went involuntarily to the flinger he carried at his waist-belt.

"A Crome!"

It was an effort for Hrityu not to go for his own flinger at sight of the enemy. He caught his breath.

"Easy," he warned. "Remember, there can be no violence here. The Market is neutral territory. Any who break this rule cannot trade."

"But why is he here?" muttered Kurwer.

The Crome had spotted them. He sauntered over, a humanoid fully a head taller than Hrityu and Kurwer. His shoulders were exaggeratedly broad, his torso slanting to a narrow waist. His bumpy, roughened skin was a deep, vivid green, making the black of his eyes all the more intimidating. Six neat crests, also black and barely a finger's breadth in height, swept over his skull and gave a grooved appearance to the pate.

Like Hrityu and Kurwer, and like most of the denizens of the desert planet, he was naked save for metal bangles on his arms and legs and belts and straps to which were hooked packs and pocket. His own flinger, a long-shafted Crome version, was slung across his shoulder. One arm hooked casually over the stock, he waggled the weapon provocatively as he approached with black eyes glinting.

His expression was one of supercilious mirth as he looked the Analane up and down. When he spoke, his voice was sharp and piercing, with a florid accent.

"What's this? Blueskins! No need to ask why you are here. You know your doom is close, and you come crawling, hoping to find something to save yourselves with."

"Why are *you* here, if not for a similar purpose?" Hrityu retorted.

The Crome affected surprise. He shifted his long flinger from one shoulder to the other, contriving to point the shaft at Kurwer and make it look as if he were about to discharge it at him. He laughed when they both flinched.

"The Crome have no need of new weapons, though I shall keep an eye on you to see you do not obtain something inconvenient to us. By order of the Ephors of Crome, I come to notify the Market Master that we wish to exterminate the blue skins altogether when we launch our main attack upon them. I am sure they will have no objection. What importance the Tlixix is a band of mould-munchers?"

Having delivered this insult to Analane eating habits—the Crome themselves lived on the pith of a spiny sandplant—the green humanoid strolled away, leaving Hrityu and Kurwer staring grimly at one another.

"Can he be telling the truth?" rasped Kurwer, aghast.

"You heard the way he just spoke of us. Blueskins, mould-munchers. I am sure the Crome are capable of it."

"But would the Tlixix give permission? To wipe out an entire race!"

"It sounds incredible," Hrityu admitted. "But above all the Tlixix like to preserve an outward appearance of authority. If it looks like the Crome will go ahead anyway . . . Yes, the Market Master may give his permission, simply so as not to be defied."

He gripped his flinger and his face set. "There is only one sure way out for us. We must make certain that we win the war!"

CHAPTER TWO

The entrance to the Pavilion of Warfare was in appearance a long grill, the gaps between whose teeth were automatic doors which shot up when touched, sliding smoothly back down again a few moments later. Having watched this mechanism operated by a lizard Grokog who disappeared inside the building, Hrityu tried it for himself. The two Analane slipped nimbly through and were faced with a vast interior.

A cantilevered roof admitted light through transparent sections. Beneath it, the cavernous space was marked out into various stands accessed by aisles. A whispering, booming noise filled the air. It was a concert of talk, of devices being demonstrated, of objects being dragged across the floor. What struck the Analane most forcibly, however, was a peculiar quality and smell to the atmosphere, making them curl up their facial membranes, giving them a feeling of discomfort.

It was moisture. There was moisture in the air.

Not much, it was true. The humidity was evaporation from a podium some distance from the entrance. There, reposing in a bath-like couch, tented in transparent curtains, lay one of the Market Masters: a Tlixix, stalks and feelers waving and twitching, the telescoping segments of his shell gleaming with a bluish sheen.

The Analane stared in awe as they timidly approached the podium. The Tlixix bore no resemblance either to lizard or humanoid: they had ruled the world long, long ago, before the Great Dehydration, when none of the desert species had existed.

In those days, it was said, water had been everywhere, floating in the sky, falling from the air, lying on the ground in vast sheets as far as the eye could see. Such a hellish world was hard to envisage, but if it could be imagined, then the Tlixix was a fitting creature to live in it. Angled over the bath-couch were pipes ending in nozzles from which atomised sprays of water hissed over it. Fortunately little of the spray drifted through the folds of the curtains. Hrityu knew that such as did was mostly recovered at night, when it condensed against the cooling walls of the building. The Market Masters were careful hoarders of the corrosive, alien substance on which their lives, and theirs alone, depended.

The bewhiskered, chitinous visage, whose eyes were no more than whitish scales, had a bleary look. Water sploshed in the bath-couch as the Tlixix leaned towards the arrivals, speaking in a voice that was hoarse and distant-sounding.

"You come to buy and sell?"

Momentarily Hrityu found that his voice had deserted him. He drew himself erect.

"We Analane are engaged in a war with the Crome, who lately have begun destroying the beds of ground-fungus which is our food. We are here to barter for weapons with which to defend ourselves against a stronger enemy."

"Is the conflict permitted?"

Hrityu hesitated. "The Market Masters were notified. No edict of denial has been issued."

"I shall check the truth of that. Meanwhile, go your way. When you have made a transaction, there is a fee to be paid. Should you wish to rent space in the pavilion to display wares of your own, the terms will be explained upon request. Do you understand all this?"

"Yes."

The Tlixix twitched a feeler and turned away. He appeared to be luxuriating in the water in which he lolled and with which he was being sprayed, even though the weird environment was all he had known since being hatched.

The Analane set off cautiously between the rows of stands, carefully inspecting everything around them. At nearly every stand a hawker boasted of the death-dealing devices that were on show there, irrespective of whether anyone was nearby to listen. On offer were flingers of various types and sizes, their innovation lying in the ingenuity of the flenchers they projected, or else in their range or speed. There was little of interest there, and Hrityu and Kurwer passed them by. They passed by, too, rolling war wagons to be hurled at an enemy spitting darts in all directions, multiple flingers trailing nets which would then contract, choking the life out of an enemy, and engines for raising such a wind that an enemy was faced with a lethal sandblast.

They were in search of something invincible. The Crome had to be defeated without question. And with them they had brought the means to pay for it: one of the greatest inventions ever—as great a step forward, possibly, as the radium motor itself.

Deeper into the pavilion stands were stocked with sample mercenary warriors, both humanoid and lizard. The Analane took no notice of these. Mercenaries could not be trusted, being liable to turn on their paymasters if they found themselves on the losing side.

New methods of war lay at the far end of the pavilion, and this was what the Analane were pinning their hopes on. They gazed bewildered at a jumble of battle machines of all shapes and sizes, until a blue-skinned lizard a head taller than Hrityu accosted them.

"You are here to buy?"

Hrityu nodded. The lizard's reply was a hiss. "Then witness our ferocious invention in action."

At his gesture his helpers set to pushing a large, heavy block of a dark material in place. Then there was aimed at it a weapon resembling some sort of giant flinger, but instead of a shaft there was what looked like a barrel or cylinder.

Two lizards withdrew to safety. A third squatted behind the weapon, and pulled a lever.

A radium motor had all the while been humming in the depths of the contraption. Now, with a rapid ratcheting noise, the barrel of the weapon rotated, hurling an incredible stream of flenchers.

The onslaught seemed endless. Before their eyes the target block was chewed to bits.

"This machine is the product of much mechanical skill," the lizard hissed smoothly. "It will annihilate a whole company of warriors. Consequently its price is high."

Stunned by the demonstration, Kurwer became excited. Hrityu, however, cautioned him to silence.

They passed on, and were accosted by a sand-coloured Grishi who spoke to them gruffly. "Curiosity-seekers are not welcome among those who innovate and invent. Is what you can offer of comparable value to what you find here?"

"What we have," Kurwer snapped, "is so extraordinary that only dire necessity persuades us to part with it!"

The Grishi inspected him, and then nodded slowly. "Perhaps you would care to see our own devastating contribution to the art of total warfare. It works by denying the enemy breathable air."

He turned and picked up a glass globe from a nearby table. It contained a mass of green crystals. "Sprayed onto a force of enemy warriors, this preparation instantly absorbs the life-giving element in the atmosphere, causing them to fall insensible. I am ready to prove its efficacy against a few prisoners we keep in the testing ground outside—if, that is, your own goods can be deemed of equal desirability."

From the adjoining stand a Grishi of a different tribe, his skin a somewhat darker orange, laughed. "My rival's chemicals are interesting, but unreliable. They do not necessarily kill the enemy, who is apt to recover later. Here, now, I have a device of a definitely lethal description: a machine which casts a tough flexible canopy over the enemy. The canopy contracts, stifling its victims. As many as a hundred may be asphyxiated together."

He indicated a balled-up rubbery object in the midst of an arrangement of rods and loaded springs. "I, too, can apply it to some prisoners I keep ready, provided there is sufficient inducement."

Kurwer drew Hrityu aside to confer. "Each of these weapons seems impressive in its own way," he said doubtfully. "What do you think? Perhaps we could obtain them all."

Sadly Hrityu shook his head. "It is the custom for the buyer of an invention to demand sole possession of it.We can offer our radiator to one party only, and I do not think any of these weapons are its equal in value."

"What could be more valuable than the survival of the Analane?"

"But nothing we have seen so far guarantees victory. The machines are large and clumsy. They could be overrun or stolen, leaving us worse off than before. It is too early to reach a decision."

They moved off, and as they did so a small slim humanoid, standing no taller than Hrityu's shoulder, sidled up. Hrityu stopped. He had not seen the stranger's like before. His skin was as black as a Gaminte's, but was covered in fine corrugations that might have been tribal markings. Most striking was the absence of any head-crest: his bald pate aroused a measure of revulsion in the two Analane. Striking too were his eyes: milky pale, and wide as if in wonderment.

"Analane," he said in a low, purring tone, "a Crome has boasted of your tribe's impending destruction. One may deduce that in military terms your position is untenable."

Hrityu replied stiffly. "That is supposition only."

The other raised a placating hand. "No doubt the Crome are much given to bluster. I am of the Toureen. We live a long way from here, within the barriers of a fifty-lang-wide crater, and so are little known. But we are not without inventiveness. For two years I have waited in this pavilion to see if anything can match what we have to offer. You have something to barter?"

"Indeed."

"May one enquire . . . ?"

"We shall reveal our device when we see something we want in exchange."

The Toureen paused before replying. "Strangely, that is also my policy."

He gestured around him. "Nothing you may see here is comparable with what I can give you. Any who possess it will win supremacy in the field of battle . . . we appear to be at an impasse, unless we can at least describe our respective goods."

"Even for that, mutual trust is necessary."

"I am ready to risk mine."

Hrityu looked down at the bald black pate of the Toureen. In his own tribe it signified emasculation, and he wondered how it could be possible to trust such a creature.

"Then you must speak first," he said.

Beckoning, the Toureen drew him down the aisle and apart from any of the stands. He looked this way and that to ensure he was not overheard, and spoke quietly.

"Our weapon achieves total disintegration of whatever it is hurled against. It can burst huge rocks asunder. It could demolish this entire pavilion in the space of a single breath."

"You make an extravagant claim," Hrityu responded, trying to picture what the Toureen was saying.

"But a true one. The world has never before seen such sudden and violent force in the service of war. It can be compared to the eruption of a volcano." He paused. "Now: tell me of your device."

"Very well, but it is not a weapon," Hrityu told him. "Our mechanics have discovered a means of long-range communication. We call it a radiator. It is able to transmit the spoken voice over great distances—we have tested it up to a hundred langs."

Seeing the look of puzzlement on the Toureen's face, he continued: "Its greatest value lies in its secrecy. Invisible radiations that can neither be seen nor heard carry the voice. It is made audible only by means of a receiving apparatus carried by the listener. Imagine, if you can, the uses this invention can be put to. Messages can be sent without a messenger, and what is more, received the instant they re dispatched."

The Toureen was evidently having trouble understanding him. And indeed the radiator was so strange, so inexplicable, that Hrityu himself sometimes had difficulty believing it. "To send a voice a hundred langs with no one in between hearing it?" the black humanoid said in mystification. "That would be most remarkable . . . "

"We do not lie. Only dire necessity persuades us to divulge this secret, as you have deduced. If you are interested in obtaining it, then I wish to see this weapon of yours."

The Toureen made up his mind. "Come with me."

He took them out of the Pavilion of Warfare and past the adjacent compound where dejected prisoners waited as targets on which to demonstrate this weapon or that to prospective customers. At the rear of the compound, ochre Yongs fought with buff lizards, Yong blades clashing with lizard prongs. Hrityu guessed them to be rival groups of mercenaries competing for a commission.

Soon they were in the humming vehicle park. Their guide showed them to a low-slung, six-wheeled carriage, and invited them to board it. They reclined uneasily on cushions piled in the box-like passenger compartment, while the Toureen seized a steering lever and yanked on a hand-grip.

The vehicle rolled forward. Careless of who stood in his path, the Toureen negotiated the concourse with skill and soon they had left the World Market behind and were heading into the plain towards the hills.

For some time the vehicle rushed over the sand, their driver offering no hint as to their destination. Suddenly he made for a clump of rocks. Behind it was a depression that, until one came suddenly upon it, remained unseen. At its bottom a small camp had been set up with two more ebon Toureen squatting beneath an awning.

The vehicle crept into the hollow and stopped. The driver got out and spoke to his tribesmen. They glanced at the Analane, then reached into the back of the awning and dragged forward an evidently heavy chest, whose lid they threw open.

"Here, if you please."

Hesitantly, Hrityu and Kurwer stepped down and approached.

The chest was filled with brown globes, nearly the size of a Toureen's head. Hrityu was reminded of the flasks of air-absorbing crystals he had seen earlier, until one was taken from the chest and he saw that a short cord dangled from it.

Their guide picked up two shields from a pile that lay nearby and handed one to each of the Analane. "These will protect you from the fragments. Now: we had best get out of the hollow."

No explanations were offered as the party scrambled up the incline, each carrying a shield and the three Toureen cradling a number of the brown spheres in their arms. At the top, some distance from the rocks, the leader called a halt.

"We shall hurl the balls at those rooks. Hide behind your shields."

The spheres were placed on the ground. Squatting behind their shields, Hrityu and Kurwer watched as the two Toureen from the camp took up a globe each and applied fire to the cords from tinder-boxes that dangled from their necks. The cords sizzled. The Toureen ran for the rocks. Peeping over his shield, Hrityu saw them hurl the globes and then come scampering back to throw themselves behind their own shields.

Instinctively he ducked. From the direction of the rock clump came a massive noise, a double blast, one a split second after the other. Hrityu had never heard anything so loud; it actually hurt his ears. Missiles were battering away at his shield, as if shot from flingers. Then something seemed to be trying to tear the shield from his grasp, and following that, fragments of rock came rattling down from the air.

When the pandemonium was over, pungent-smelling smoke came drifting in their direction. Hrityu dared a look. He stared stupefied.

Part of the rock clump had vanished.

"Again!" the Toureen leader ordered.

The ritual was repeated. Again came the titanic blasts, the fusillade of rock fragments, the buffeting wind.

Even more of the rock clump had been demolished. Chunks of it lay about the desert floor.

The Toureen waited until everyone had climbed to his feet before speaking. "We call the substance *eruptionite*," he explained. "The recipe is fairly simple, merely a matter of mixing certain purified chemicals in the right proportions. When ignited, the mixture erupts as you have seen. The force of the eruption is greatly increased if the mixture is confined in a strong, solid shell, and this, of course, is also a convenient way of delivering it. The shells can be made to any size—small enough to be hand-flung, or so big that only specially made flingers could hurl them. As you have just witnessed, eruptionite will even tear apart stone fortifications. The Crome will be blown to bits."

Hrityu pondered. "Do you undertake to provide us with the mixture itself, or merely the formula?"

"We can supply a sufficient amount of eruptionite to give you a breathing space, thereafter you must manufacture it for yourselves. By the usual protocol, we also promise not to sell it to any other tribe."

Again Hrityu pondered. Kurwer spoke up.

"Since this weapon is so potent, why do you not wish to preserve it for your own use?"

"We Toureen are not accustomed to engaging in war. Our crater walls have so far been sufficient discouragement to invaders, and they are so massive that not even eruptionite could breach them My race delights in new knowledge, and therefore we are willing to impart this secret if in so doing we gain another that is equally remarkable."

"You shall have your wish," Hrityu said confidently, "for this is indeed the weapon we seek. The time has come to exchange names. I am Hrityu, of the Analane. My companion is named Kurwer."

The other drew his small slim bulk erect. "I am Nussmussa, of the Toureen. Now as to this radiator . . . you mentioned a range of one hundred langs. How may this be put to the test?"

"One hundred langs is perhaps rather too much to demonstrate easily," Hrityu admitted doubtfully. "What do you suggest?"

"You have the apparatus at the market?"

"Yes."

"Then we shall put the transmitting device in your vehicle, and the receiving device in our vehicle. One of my party will accompany you while we drive for one half of a day in opposite directions, and will attempt to speak to me at intervals. When the sun reaches its zenith, we shall return."

Hrityu nodded. "That is acceptable. Let us return to the market, and we will show you the radiator."

The warm breeze blew in the Analane's faces as they rode in the Toureen vehicle. Hrityu tried to calm his elation, reminding himself that there was still much to be done. Transport would have to be arranged for the initial supply of eruptionite before the Crome staged their main attack. Also, how difficult might it be to find and purify the chemicals needed for its manufacture? This would have to be talked out with Nussmussa.

Then again, there were the Tlixix to deal with, and their fee to be arranged.

Hrityu reflected that it might be worth applying to the Pavilion of Audience to try to forestall the Crome's petition.

At his direction Nussmussa sped into the market, wheeled into the vehicle park and flashed past the lines of carriages to halt beside the Analane rover. Hrityu and Kurwer stepped down and went to the rear of their vehicle, opening the hidden compartment where they had secreted their precious apparatus.

He blinked as he pulled up the metal panel. He was not sure that he could believe his eyes. Then a horrified sound escaped from his throat. His eyes had not deceived him.

Their invaluable cargo, the radiator and its accompanying receiver upon which the survival of the Analane depended, was gone!

CHAPTER THREE

Poised in an orbit synchronous with the planet's rotation, the twin speculae of an interferometric telescope looked down from opposite ends of a mile-long extensible rod. Their slightly different images, processed by point-to-point comparison, gave Messrs. Krabbe and Bouche an excellent view of the World Market far below them.

Karl Krabbe twiddled a knob beneath the viewplate. The scene, currently bird's-eye, shifted and tilted until it was as though one stood on the ground amid the inhabitants. The processor made a fair job of the representation, though the deduced facial features tended to be vague and fuzzy. He focused on a drama in cameo: two thin blue humanoids gesticulated excitedly to a smaller black humanoid. They had opened up the rear of a wheeled vehicle.

He turned to Boris Bouche. "It's the nearest thing to a town on the whole damned planet! You only find camps and villages anywhere else."

"That's because towns are markets, essentially, and this is the only market they have." Bouche's voice had an acid quality, easily given to sarcasm. "God, Karl, I have to remind you of enough. Don't you remember your economics?"

"Sure I remember," Krabbe retorted testily. "What makes you think I don't?"

Karl Krabbe was a barrel of a man, his large, ruddy face seeming always about to break into some anguished pronouncement, leaving it lined and anxious. He dressed carelessly and tended to slouch. His partner, Boris Bouche, slender and tall, was neat and compact by comparison, but the dapper impression did not extend to his face. The wide slash of his mouth and the close-set eyes gave him a predatory look. He stepped forward, peering over Krabbe's shoulder at the plate.

"Here comes one of the bosses."

Krabbe had panned the focus to the main concourse. One of the lobster-like creatures was being moved from one pavilion to another. A transparent tent covered the motorised dray. Within it, water sprays asperged the bulky, shelled passenger. There was something lordly about the beast's slow progress through the throng, whiskery stalks waving above the foot traffic.

"If we do any business here, it's his sort we'll be dealing with," Bouche said.

Krabbe grunted. "I mostly like crustaceans in a well-blended sauce."

"Crustaceans? Yes, I suppose that's close enough, though you could say he is to a crayfish what we are to . . . well, there isn't any mammal as brainless as a crayfish. What we are to a newt, maybe."

"And on a desert planet. It's amazing."

"Not really. It's just that they're smart. Wouldn't you say so, Spencer?"

He craned his neck to the planetologist who stood at the back of the room. Spencer nodded, and came forward.

"Yes, sir. There's not much doubt that this planet was watery once, perhaps as recently as fifty thousand Earth years ago. Then the water suddenly vanished, for some reason. Castaneda is working on the data now.

"The crustacean-like creatures were the dominant intelligent species of the time, and as far as we can tell they are the only one to have survived the calamity—except, presumably, for whatever fauna or flora they keep as food. Instead, a desert biosphere has arisen, one that doesn't need water. That the lobsters, as you call them, have managed to maintain some sort of dominance despite their small numbers is a tribute to their tenacity, I would say. They own all the free water on the planet, and conserve it with great care. I imagine they make good any losses by paying other species to process whatever tiny amounts can be extracted from plants and the dead bodies of desert creatures.

"That market is the secret of their power. They created it and they manage it, as the only real centre of trade on the whole planet. It gives them their wealth and their prestige, and makes it possible for them to impose their own conditions on anyone who wants to come there. Physically they could be wiped out overnight, but they've been there right through the evolution of the desert species, whose history they have practically managed, and that gives them enormous psychological pull. They rule by nerve."

"That's what I don't understand," Krabbe complained. "There's a whole crop of intelligent species now. We probably haven't even seen them all yet! How could that happen in only fifty thousand years?"

"Fifty thousand is the lower limit, sir. It could be as much as a quarter of a million, though that's an equally ridiculous period from our point of view. I suspect the losters had a hand in that, too. They needed servant species to help them survive. To that we can add that there must be a terrific rate of mutation. There's an awful lot of radium down there. They even use it to power their engines."

"Were you surprised to find a waterless biology, Spencer?" Bouche asked.

"Yes sir, I was. We picked up a couple of specimens. Seeing as how they evolved from water-based animals in the first place, the body chemistry is pretty ingenious. Their bodies do hold tiny quantities of water, but it's held in a glycerine-like gel. They don't perspire or excrete liquid waste. Their blood *doesn't circulate*, if you can believe it. Oxygen and nutrients and all the rest migrate chemically through gelatinous blood, the molecules being passed hand to hand through the gel, so to speak. I'd swear it was impossible if I hadn't seen it."

Krabbe stared at the interferoscope plate, where the 'lobster' was disappearing inside the building which was the market overlords' special retreat and where, presumably, they could be permanently drenched in water.

"Tenacity," he murmured. "That's what those old boys have got, all right. So that's what we'll call this planet, okay? *Tenacity*."

"All right, if you want," Bouche said sourly. "*Tenacity* it is."

*

The food tray supported nonchalantly by the flat of one hand, Joanita Serstos walked the corridors of the gogetter ship with an easy, lank stride. She smiled on coming to the locked titanium alloy door.

Licking her lips, she fingered the lock tab.

"Hi, honey," she said. "How goes it?"

"Hello, Jo," a good-natured, if weary, male voice answered. "Why don't you come in?"

A miniature oval image had appeared on the door. It showed the interior of the prison cell. Roncie Reaul Northrop lounged in an easy chair, one foot plonked on an occasional table. She tut-tutted to see how careless he still was with the furnishings, despite her admonishments. There was a big coffee stain on the carpet. The place was a mess.

He looked up from the book he was reading and smiled in greeting as she walked in, letting the door swing shut behind her. The vidset in the corner was switched on; involuntarily she glanced at the living, glowing flesh-tones it showed.

He followed her gaze and his smile became broader. It was a tape of her visit the day before. Their naked bodies were working away, her fleshy buttocks gyrating and nearly filling the screen.

She watched interestedly for a few moments, then waved her hand to turn the set off. She swept Northrop's feet off the table to make room and laid down the tray.

"Really, Roncie."

"Only trying to bring a blush to those maidenly features."

"No chance."

She lifted the cover off the tray to arrange the meal the way she knew he liked it. Knife, fork, mustard and chile sauce for the steak, chopsticks and soya sauce for the bowl of fried rice and prawns, a gold-plated spoon for the tangy lemon marsala custard. Northrop breathed deeply. The tang of the chile sauce somehow reminded him of her. Her skin was copper, almost orange, her face high-cheekboned. What he liked especially were her muscular, lithe legs and her long sexy stride.

"Tell me something. Did Krabbe & Bouche order you to keep me serviced while I'm in the brig? Or is that a bonus?"

"Shut up and eat."

Patiently she began picking up the books that were scattered about, placing them back in the shelves. She smoothed out the bed and vacuumed the carpet. By the time he had dealt with the steak, she was cleaning off the coffee stain with a remover pad.

There was more than idle curiosity to his question. She had never consented to take a tumble with him until his incarceration. It could be out of sympathy of course, but equally it was possible his masters wanted him in a receptive frame of mind. After all, she was a Krabbe & Bouche bondwoman, one of about fifty bonded people on the gogetter ship. The entire staff, the entire ship's complement, was bonded—Krabbe & Bouche did not recruit staff on any other basis. They wanted reliability.

"Doesn't it bother you that K&B's licence to operate has been revoked?" he asked. "Technically that ends your bonded status. You don't have to do any of this."

She snorted. "A fat lot the Stellar Commission means out here."

He could see she was satisfied with her lot. Generally speaking Krabbe & Bouche had little to worry about as regards staff loyalty, the whole position of bonded employees being legally ambiguous. A bonded person was a semi-slave, required to obey his employers without question. That was apt to remain the case in practice—if not in law—even when the employer was in breach of his obligations.

Roncie Northrop had tried to go by the book. Learning of the revocation order the Stellar Commission had issued after Krabbe & Bouche transgressed the Non-Interference Law on Sesquielta, he had jumped ship. It was his philosophy not to back losers. And in any case he had come to dislike the rapacious partners he served.

He had reckoned without Boris Bouche's meticulous point-twisting manipulations. At that time they had been docked in Durovia, where it was difficult to recruit trained people. Northrop had not formally applied to be released from his bond; Bouche posted him as an absconder.

On Durovia the proctors followed procedure unimaginatively. The police had found Northrop and despite his protests had brought him straight back to the ship. He had been in the brig ever since.

"You do know there's a Pursuit Order?" he persisted.

"Oh sure, and they'll send a ship and find us too. Anyway, so what?"

She was right. The Stellar Commission's casual way of doing things meant it was unlikely the *Enterprise* would ever be tracked down.

He began raking fried rice into his mouth with quick motions. To be fair, Krabbe & Bouche probably weren't a lot worse than most gogetters. All of them hated the Non-Interference Law; profit was all they cared about. Provided they went far enough into deep space they could flout the law for long enough to make it worthwhile.

"There, that's better," Joanita said after her tidying-up efforts. "You live like a pig, Roncie."

"I'm penned up like one."

"It's for your own good, Roncie. Bouche could have punished you. Instead he jut put you under restriction."

"For K & B's good is what you mean!" Northrop protested plaintively. "Bouche had me thrown in here so I wouldn't get a chance to renounce my bond. Not that he'd have taken a blind bit of notice if I did— that's why I jumped ship in the first place. By the way, are we still in orbit?"

"Yes, over the little yellow planet. There's been a geological report."

"And?"

She shrugged. "I hear there might be work. You'll be needed."

Northrop frowned thoughtfully. As a nuclear engineer he was on Castaneda's geological team. "So they have nuclear power on this planet? They want help with some geo-engineering?"

She giggled. "You could say that. Don't worry, pretty boy. It's all out of your hands, anyway."

He dipped the golden spoon into the bowl of marsala. "Here, come and share this with me."

She came closer, bending as he lifted the spoon to her. He slipped his hand up the inside of her well-tensioned thigh. Beneath her short smock she wasn't wearing anything.

The yellow cream was thick on her lips. She licked it off, and allowed him to tug her down beside him. They ate the marsala together, mouth to mouth, lips twining, passing it back and forth. By the time it was gone the work-smock was up to her shoulders. He panted as he swallowed the last of the sweet.

"Wait a sec," she said. She jumped up, took a pace and waved her hand. The light over the vidcamera blinked on.

"Something more for your library," she grinned as she rejoined him.

Northrop didn't say anything. Where his mouth was, he couldn't say anything.

*

Castaneda, the leader of the Geological Team, entered the conference room accompanied by Runkfoh, his assistant. He carried a sheaf of papers under his arm. His florid features looked troubled.

Krabbe turned, pleased by his early arrival. "Good work, Castaneda. What's the news?"

For answer Castaneda laid out a large map on the table in the centre of the room. Krabbe and Bouche both came to look at it. It was a geological surveyor's map of the planet, done on a Mercator projection.

"Much what we expected, Partner Krabbe, sir. The planet below us—"

"Tenacity," Krabbe interrupted.

"Sir?"

"Tenacity. That's what we decided to call it."

"Yes, sir. Well, uh, Tenacity is, in its own small way, a freak planet. A small enough planet—smaller than Mars. It has an unusually thin crust, and beneath that, the mantle is in layers. The top layer is also unusual: made up of a porous rock of a structure I confess I haven't come across before. On any other world it would have got compressed by now and would have lost its porosity. It also contains fracture zones, similar to the tectonic plates found in the crust of many larger planets."

He waved his hand over the map. "As you know already, Tenacity had surface water once. It was a one-continent world: this one big continent here, and one big ocean, just like Earth used to have long ago, before our mother continent broke up. The ocean on the side of the planet opposite the continent was very deep. It had worn away the crust and lay on the mantle. However, there was enough pressure on the mantle to stop it absorbing any water, though there must have been enough heat convection to make for a pretty warm, balmy ocean.

"Then the catastrophe happened. A stability that had existed for millions, maybe billions of years was disturbed. I think it was probably due to tidal influence from the inward planet, which is bigger than Tenacity and approaches within fifteen million miles. The fracture plates slipped. Some of the pressure on the mantle zone under the deep ocean was eased. The rock became like an expanding sponge. The seawater drained into like it was going down a plughole."

He shook his head wonderingly. "It must have been really sudden. All in a few years, tens of years at the most. The drainage region lies under a mile of sand now.

"Whatever small amounts of water were left will have taken longer to disappear. First it will have evaporated, and then gradually been disassociated by solar radiation, the hydrogen rising to the top of the atmosphere."

"So you were right," Krabbe breathed. "It's still there!"

"Right under their feet, though they don't know it."

Bouche spoke, glancing ferally at Castaneda. "The point is, can we get it back again?"

Castaneda nodded. He stabbed his finger at another part of the survey map. "This faultline here is what it's all about. It kept the water up top once and it can do it again. If we put down a few strategically placed shock tubes we can lever the plates back into opposition again. The pressure will come back on. The rock won't be able to hold all that water. It will come squirting up to fill the old ocean bed. It will rain again, there'll be rivers, lakes, inland seas. Plenty of shoreline for the lobster people."

"Shoreline. That's what they must like."

"Yes. Of course, the water will be rather warm to begin with. Up to a hundred degrees. Most of it's steam right now."

Bouche stared at the map. "Why don't I see your shock tubes placed?"

"We shall need to survey the area in detail, do some drilling. I suggest Runkfoh takes charge of that, sir. Northrop's experience will also be valuable."

"Runkfoh?" Krabbe said suspiciously. "What's wrong with you doing it, Castaneda?"

Castaneda became diffident. "As you may recall, sir, I am prone to cancers. There's a lot of radium down there. It's very carcinogenic. May I request that I be excused from going down on the surface?"

"Is that all? Don't be a sissy, Castaneda. Use radpaint, that'll take care of it." Krabbe looked aggravated.

"Radpaint isn't completely effective, sir," Castaneda pleaded.

"Then you can get cured. You've been cured before, haven't you?" Krabbe waved his hand dismissively. "Get on with the job. If we make a deal, I want to be able to move fast. And you can take Northrop from the brig."

The picture of defeat, the geological engineer took up his map and folded it among his papers. He nodded to Runkfoh. The two men left.

Krabbe went back to the viewplate. "You know, Boris," he said, "those lobsters must have a terrible hunger. They must feel a terrible frustration. They were clever enough to survive the dehydration, so it's obvious they have a lot of experience and a healthy urge to dominate. If Tenacity should get its water back they'll be in their element again. They'll be able to proliferate, restore their former grandeur. We can give them heaven! What won't they pay for it?"

"As to that," Bouche said with a scowl, "I suspect we'll find they're pretty smart traders."

"We'll stick them with a contract, don't worry about that. Equal partners in a whole world! Why, the radium alone—what was the quote on radium, last you heard? Our own empire! After all, it's an offer they practically can't refuse."

There was a cough from Spencer. Nervously, he spoke. "What about the dehydrate species, sir? Giving Tenacity its water back will hardly do them much good. It will almost certainly kill most of them, if not all."

"Oh, they're just savages, Spencer, the sort that die out on thousands of planets once there's any progress. Why, take a look here—"

He twisted knobs. A tall, thin, green desert warrior came into view. "See that weapon he carries? With a stock like a rifle, only instead of a barrel it fires that funny curved blade? It's a flenching blade, and it spins as it flies through the air. Its purpose is to carve as much flesh from the bone as possible." He shook his head with a show of moral disapproval. "Weapons as horrific as that are outlawed on every civilised world."

Spencer was relatively new to the staff and this was his first time on a gogetter ship—his first experience as a bondman, in fact. Krabbe spoke to him affably, condescendingly. It pleased him to be avuncular.

"Of course," Bouche commented, "it's probably the best way to be sure of killing someone who doesn't bleed."

Bravely Spencer said, "What I question is the legality of it, sir, not the morality. Interfering with the geography and climate of an alien planet, not to say the culture, to the extent of species extermination . . . "

"The desert dwellers are a biological sport," Krabbe said shortly. "They resulted from a natural catastrophe. The lobsters are the authentic owners of Tenacity, and we'll have their approval."

"I only hope the Stellar Commission sees it that way, sir. I don't need to remind you of the penalties."

"That's nothing for you to worry your head about, Spencer," Krabbe told him firmly. "Only Partner Bouche and myself are legally liable for the orders we give."

"Yes sir." Spencer sat biting his lip.

Boris Bouche took over his partner's argument, leaning towards the younger man, one foot on a desk rail, one arm resting on his bended knee. The stance made him seem even more wolf-like. "You see, son, the Stellar Commission is maybe five, even ten years behind us—if they find us at all. By that time we'll have transformed this planet. The new weather pattern will have had time to settle down. There won't be anything left of the de-hydrate species you talk about. And we'll have a solid contract to give us mining, manufacturing and trading rights. How could anybody put oceans on an arid world?" He chuckled, genuinely amused. "The worst they'll be able to stick on us is operating without a licence."

"That's right!" Krabbe joined in triumphantly. "And we'll have a *fait accompli*. The firm of Krabbe & Bouche will be in business again!"

CHAPTER FOUR

Black Gamintes from the Trusk region were what the Tlixix used as the market's slender guard force. On finding the radiator missing, Hrityu had immediately rushed to find one.

The Tlixix had been quickly informed. Hrityu expected them to be very angry indeed. The market was a sacrosanct place and neither violence nor theft were permitted there. The Tlixix knew very well that their credibility depended on the observance of those rules.

Just the same, the Analane trembled with nervousness as they stood before the two Tlixix who were to investigate the case. For one of them was none other than Rherrsherrsh, the Market Master himself.

They had not hesitated to accuse the hated Crome who earlier had taunted them. He therefore stood by their side, as well as Nussmussa the Toureen, all surrounded by red-eyed Gamintes fingering their flingers, spiked silver hair glinting in the poor light.

The interior of the Pavilion of Audience was maintained more for the comfort of the Tlixix than for any other race. Out of deference to the petitioners the two market lords were ensconced in their usual tented bath couches, yet water still hung on the air, and the humanoids all experienced various degrees of physical discomfort.

Rherrsherrsh was an aging Tlixix, his antlers turning from white to greenish-grey with his advancing years. He bent towards Hrityu.

"This occurrence is of the utmost rarity, as well as of great gravity," he said in the hoarse tones of his race. The Market Master's displeasure was almost palpable. "Why do you accuse this Crome?"

"Our reasons are all too obvious, Market Master," Hrityu began. "The Crome are at war with the Analane and are embarked on a campaign of extermination, from no other motive than blind hatred! We—"

A deep laugh from the Crome interrupted him. "No motive. Market Masters, the Analane are invading our territory. They have planted beds of their vile mould there and our own gardens of spine-plant have become infected with it. We shall die of starvation unless they are defeated."

"New beds must be planted in new places!" Kurwer shouted excitedly. "The old beds do not stay productive."

"It's them or us, Market Master," the Crome rumbled.

The antlers of both Tlixix waved in disapproval. "The conflict between you is not the subject of this hearing."

Rherrsherrsh admonished. "Analane, continue with your accusation."

"We have brought to the market an invention of great importance, which we hoped to exchange for some new weapons with which to defend our race," Hrityu continued evenly. "Clearly this execrable Crome feared that our mission would be successful. Why, he even admitted to us that he is here to spy on us. Obviously, he stole our equipment to prevent that."

The Crome's lustrous black eyes shone. "We Crome are not so foolish," he said. "We fear the Analane not at all, whatever weapons they procure. Besides, to commit this offence would risk the expulsion of my entire race from the market! Would I be so rash?" His green arm stabbed out at the Analane, his finger pointing. "I will suggest a more evident truth, market masters. The Analane had nothing with which to trade in the first place. This accusation of theirs is a ruse to bring the Crome into disfavour. They think it will somehow save their tribe from the annihilation which is their due!"

"It is indeed improbable that anyone would dare to steal on ground hallowed by the Tlixix," Rherrsherrsh declared. Water sploshed and he reared intimidatingly over the humanoids. "What is the nature of this supposed invention?"

Hrityu hesitated. But he realized he had little choice but to reveal all.

"We call it a radiator. Through it, any sound including the spoken word can be conveyed for a distance of up to one hundred langs."

There was silence, until the second Tlixix hoarsed into the conversation. "Useful perhaps if one is a hundred langs away. But is not such a vast noise unduly painful for anyone closer by?"

"The sounds are not made any louder," Hrityu explained patiently. "They are heard only by whoever possesses a receiving apparatus. That is what makes the invention so useful, since messages sent that way are heard only by one's friends and allies."

Rherrsherrsh turned to his companion. "Is that possible?" he husked.

"I doubt it," the other replied in a gravelly tone. He addressed Hrityu. "How does it work?"

Hrityu dithered, wondering how to put over so technical a matter. Kurwer came to his rescue.

"It creates sound of a subtle kind, which the ears cannot hear," he said. "We call it radiation. It is far-reaching, like sunlight."

"One can see it, then? See it but not hear it?"

Kurwer replied slowly, after a pause. "No, one cannot see it."

The pattering of water was the only sound to be heard. Hrityu rubbed his eyes, which the humidity had made sore.

The Crome chuckled. "If these Analane could invent machinery as well as they invent lies then we Crome might indeed have something to fear! Sound that cannot be heard, because it is light—except that it cannot be seen! Such soundless, invisible light describes their machine very well, because neither of them exist!"

Suddenly Rherrsherrsh turned to Nussmussa the Toureen. "Is it true you made an offer for this device?"

"Yes, Market Master."

"Did you see it in operation?"

Nussmussa glanced at the Analane fretfully. "No, I did not. I did not see it at all, and the bargain was agreed only in principle. They took me to see the device, but it was not there."

"More trickery!" the Crome jeered. "They duped this poor creature from a distant land so as to lend their story a semblance of credibility!"

"The radiator is real!" Kurwer burst out. "Our enemy the Crome stole it!"

Hrityu realized how badly the exchange was going. "Market Master," he stuttered, "this device could be of great use to the Tlixix. It would enable messages to be passed instantly between the water refuges. We would gladly donate it in return for protection."

"Then why did you *not* offer it to the Tlixix?" Rherrsherrsh retorted, with thunderous hoarseness.

Hrityu could not find a reply. The idea had been considered, but though the Tlixix liked to promulgate the idea that they could control all wars in the world, it was doubtful if their word alone could actually prevent one. The elders of the Analane had decided that the most likely outcome of such an offer was that the Tlixix would appropriate the device and then encourage the extermination of the Analane to give themselves a monopoly of it.

The two masters conferred together in rustles and clicks, faces almost touching, placed wetly against the fabric of their water-tents. Then Rherrsherrsh swung back to loom over the humanoids.

"There is too little evidence to support either version of events," he husked. "The defence offered by the Crome, however, is more plausible than the complaint laid by the Analane, and we find in favour of the Crome. The making of a false accusation infringes the laws of the market. The race of the Analane is barred from dealing here henceforth."

"That's not fair!" Kurwer cried out.

The massive crustacean head, ancient and hoary, bent low over the Analane. This was the first time they had seen a Tlixix so close. The wet shell, the four tiny, white, expressionless eyes, the ever-restless feelers and whiskers, presented a vision that struck them both to the bone.

"We—we must be given time to search for our machine!" Hrityu stuttered. "To prove that it exists!"

The Tlixix deliberated. "Three days are allowed for that Purpose. The Gamintes, too, are ordered to search for the supposed apparatus during that time. To that end you will give them a complete physical description—if you can."

The audience was at an end. All humanoids, even the Gamintes, were by now breathing with difficulty in the vapour-laden air, enclosed as it was by trickling walls and a moistly shining floor. Yet as they left the pavilion the Analane could only feel despair, despite the physical relief.

"They are against us!" Kurwer wailed. "What can we do?"

Hrityu shook his head sadly. "I do not think they believe the Crome's word more than ours. They are driven by expediency. They may already have given the Crome permission to exterminate us, and wish to retain their support."

The potential value of the radiator, he reflected, did not seem to have occurred to them. Or—a startling thought—did Rherrsherrsh think the Crome *had* stolen it, and would give it to them?

Nussmussa and the Crome departed in opposite directions. A Gaminte approached, questioning them on the appearance of the radiator. The jet-black creature spoke in a polite voice and ventured no opinion of his own. His face was blank with concentration as Hrityu described the apparatus.

"Something that size wouldn't be easy to hide, unless it's been smashed to pieces," he said finally. "I suggest you search the market yourselves, since our own efforts will be scant. Remember, though—no fighting."

He turned and strode away. Hrityu and Kurwer stood together on the sand, wondering how they could ever face their co-tribesmen now.

CHAPTER FIVE

Roncie Reaul Northrop was not sure whether to be pleased or disappointed when his cell door opened and he saw standing there, not a sexually receptive Joanita Serstos, but Johnny Castaneda.

"Hello, Roncie. You're back on the team."

Castaneda stepped into the cell. He looked tired and depressed. Northrop put down the book he had been reading. "What gives, Johnny?"

Finding a chair, the geological team leader sat down wearily. "Didn't Joanita keep you informed? Oh, we have a job to do. Pretty routine technically, but K & B will sure get it in the neck if they're ever found out. How are you for radioactivity by the way? I've had such a lot of cancer . . . "

"Who hasn't?" Northrop said with a shrug. "I've had it three times myself." It was something everybody got now and then, if they spent much time in space.

"I'm practically a garden for carcinomata. The doc's told me to avoid getting them in future, if I can." Castaneda sighed. "Well, come on, Roncie, I'll give you the details."

Northrop glanced round the cell, his home of the past few weeks, before they left. Briefly he wondered if Joanita would be as accommodating towards him now he was out.

They made their way to Castaneda's office. On the wall was pinned a lithographic map, presumably of the planet the *Enterprise* was orbiting. The word TENACITY had been inked at the top of the sheet. Castaneda began to fill him in on the planet's remarkable recent history, and what their employers were planning.

"Our part's fairly simple," he finished. "We're to go down and do some test drilling and some seismic stuff, and then drill the shafts. Meanwhile the shock bombs will be put together up here in the *Enterprise*. K & B will make contact with the lobsters in person and open negotiations. When we get the word we lower the tubes and get the hell out while they go off."

"K & B are going to leave the ship to their bondpeople?"

"O'Rourke will be in charge. He's absolutely dependable. And they'll put a lock on the stardrive, of course."

"Of course."

Mildly appalled by what he had just heard, Northrop began totting up a mental list of the crimes Krabbe & Bouche were about to commit.

"I suppose he's got Shelley working on all this," he said.

"Sure." Shelley was the firm's bonded lawyer, and a joke to the rest of the staff. 'Now then, Shelley, what's the law on so-and-so?' 'Whatever you say it is, Partner Krabbe, Partner Bouche, sirs!'

Castaneda went on: "Take the law against using nuclear technology on a planet that hasn't already developed it. On Tenacity they use naturally occurring radium to power small engines. Shelley argues that makes the natives nuclear engineers! In fact they might just as well be using coal. And so on all down the line. According to Shelley we won't be undertaking planetary alteration at all. We're simply rectifying an inconvenient climatic deviation."

"In which some dozens of intelligent species will be wiped out."

The door banged open. Krabbe and Bouche burst in. They seemed to be in high spirits. For a moment Northrop thought they were drunk.

Their faces were bronze with radpaint, the standard precaution when going into a high radiation area. More extraordinary was their apparel. They had bedecked themselves in burnouses, the loose, flowing hooded cloaks once worn in hot deserts on Earth.

Bouche caught sight of Northrop. "Ah, there you are. Learned your lesson, I hope?"

Northrop drew himself up. "Sir, I wish to protest. I was on the point of renouncing my bond in Duravia, as is my right. I should not be here."

Krabbe stared at him as though he were mad. Bouche answered.

"But you *didn't* renounce your bond, Northrop. You jumped ship instead. We can hardly have that. If you had followed legal procedures, of course, then everything would be different."

Northrop listened incredulously to this last statement.

"In the event, you are here, so let's see you work with a will," Bouche finished.

"And suppose I refuse to work?"

Again Krabbe stared. "You want to renounce your bond *now*? You want *off*?" He laughed, and his eyes went to the map of Tenacity. "You might not find the local taverns to your liking."

Northrop swallowed. At least he had made his point, he thought.

Krabbe swung to him, adopting the paternalistic tone he had used earlier on Spencer. "You should be thanking heaven to be on this jaunt,

Northrop. This planet is a one-off. Everybody will get a share of the profit. The firm of Krabbe and Bouche knows how to take care of its bondpeople."

An embarrassed Castaneda put in a word. "Northrop is just a little confused from his time in the brig, sir. He'll be all right. I was just explaining the job to him."

"Well, I hope you'll be able to put in a good report on his conduct, Castaneda. Partner Bouche and I are descending to the surface now. Spencer says Tenacity has a world language, imposed by the lobsters as the dehydrate species evolved. We'll spend a few days in the market learning it, then we'll make contact. Is your team ready to move?"

"The equipment is being checked now, sir."

"Don't be too long about it. We want that work done on time."

They lurched out of the door, as if on their way to a fancy dress party.

"Better get your radpaint on, Roncie," Castaneda said.

His voice was laden with gloom.

*

Half an hour later, painted up, Northrop was surreptitiously sidling from the communications room. He stopped, blinking in embarrassment, on seeing Joanita Serstos turn the corner into the corridor.

"Well, hello, Joanita."

She halted, confronting him.

He forced a smile. She offered none in return. Instead, her expression was severe.

"What were you doing in the communications room?"

He banged the door shut behind him. "Looking for Spencer. Somebody told me I'd find him here."

"Neither Spencer nor you are allowed in there. It's out of bounds to everyone except the partners and O'Rourke. In fact, how did you get in?"

She stepped forward and tugged on the door handle. The door held.

"It was open when I got here," Roncie said casually. He reached up and touched her hair. "Anyway, I'm glad to run into you. I have to be down on the surface in an hour. How about twenty minutes on my bunk?"

She twisted away from his searching hands. "No way. In any case I'm on duty."

Joanita's voice was icy. He fell back. "I get it. And your duties have been changed, eh? I suppose I had Bouche to thank for everything after all."

"What makes you think I want to make love to someone wearing radpaint?"

Her excuse was unconvincing. The change in her manner was too obvious.

While he was in the brig the thought that she was being sent to him along with the food hadn't bothered him. Now, for some reason, it did.

"Okay, Joanita. See you when I get back."

Disgruntled, he made his way towards the bay where the ferry was being loaded up for departure.

CHAPTER SIX

There was something about the view that Karl Krabbe saw through the slatted window of his and Boris Bouche's lodging that was nudging at his memory. Along the main market concourse traders of a dozen races and colours, lizard and humanoid, passed to and fro between airy pavilions constructed of metal and coloured glass. It was kaleidoscopic, but also barbarically warlike. There was no one who did not seem to carry a weapon of some sort, and mostly the various tribesmen were naked except for bracelets, bangles, straps and belts.

The lighter had put Krabbe and Bouche down a few miles out in the desert. They had ridden in on a balloon-tyred vehicle that did not look at all out of place in the market's parking lot, and had sought out a room in one of the accommodation blocks, transferring their supplies from the dune buggy mostly at night.

No one had taken the least bit of notice of them. In appearance the aliens from another world were apparently not particularly unusual.

Suddenly the comparison that had been niggling at the back of his mind popped into his consciousness. He turned to his partner, a broad grin on his face.

"Eh, Boris! Barsoom!"

Bouche had just finished his daily contact with O'Rourke and was folding up the communicator's dish aerial. "What?"

"We should have called this world Barsoom! That's what it's like."

Bouche stared blankly.

"You know!" Krabbe urged. "Edgar Rice Burroughs! His name for Mars."

Krabbe's preoccupation with the 20th century writer was known to Bouche, but he had never read any of his work himself.

"Is that so? Well, I just told O'Rourke the language is now about adequate. Maybe we should make a move tomorrow."

Krabbe closed the window slate, shutting out the sunlight, leaving the room illuminated only by the radium-energised fluorescent patch on the ceiling. In the greenish glow their living space was little more than a large cell, meant to accommodate visiting tribesmen to the most perfunctory of standards, and now crammed with stores and equipment.

For the past three local days they had eavesdropped continuously in various parts of the market with directional microphones and hidden cameras. At length the language machine had produced its miracle, comparing sound, gesture and situation to build up a usable vocabulary. Krabbe and Bouche could now wear earplugs which would receive Tenacity speech and convert it into Terra standard. Disks worn at the base of the throat, kept in place by neckbands, likewise converted their speech to that of Tenacity, at the same time damping the original voice with cancelling anti-sound.

Now the time had come to meet with this world's controllers. Krabbe had to admit he was intrigued.

"Okay," he said. "We'll find out how to gain an audience with the— the 'Tlixix'—tomorrow."

He was interrupted by the slap of bare feet on the metal floor in the corridor. The door was suddenly shoved forcibly inward. Three black, fierce-eyed Gamintes charged into the room. One of them held on a leash a purple salamander-like creature the size of a small dog, but with six scrabbling legs.

Krabbe and Bouche retreated. The salamander creature rushed about the room, towing its keeper after it, uttering sneezing noises and scratching at the food crates. Then it began butting its head against one of the four water drums in the corner.

The Gamintes glared about them, fingering their flingers. Krabbe picked up a translator plug and began fitting it into his ear. One of the Gamintes knocked his arm away, sending the plug flying. But not before he had caught his first few harsh words.

"There is water in this room! You have been stealing water!"

The explanation came to Krabbe. He or Bouche should have thought of it before, he told himself. It was logical that the Tlixix would breed an animal capable of sniffing out the stuff that obsessed them most. The market was probably patrolled by the beasts, to locate any leaks in their system. Their noses were sensitive enough, evidently, to smell the small amount the Earthmen had been using.

A second Gaminte knelt at the water drum and after a few moments succeeded—to Krabbe's surprise—in fathoming the screw cap. He recoiled as the cap came off, then screwed it on tight.

Bouche edged towards a DE beamer, but he never reached it. There was shouting from the Gaminte. Lean, rubbery, amazingly strong arms seized the Earthmen, who were swiftly propelled from the accommodations house. Standing in the sun was a vehicle that was little more than a platform on fragile caterpillar tracks.

Krabbe and Bouche managed to raise the hoods of their burnouses before, ungraciously, they were heaved aboard it.

*

The Hydrorium was a large metal building, clad in white glass which made it dazzling to look upon. The Pavilion of Audience that confronted it was, however, the smallest in the Market. Entrance was through a circular doorway which irised open. Not until they were in the short tunnel behind it, and the door had closed, did a second door open ahead of them.

"It's a vapour lock," Bouche said admiringly. "They're taking us to the lobsters. Hell, Karl, do you realize something? This planet is as alien to them as it is to us!"

Krabbe did not answer. They were in a dimly lit hall, the walls running with moisture, the floor wet and slippery. Some distance off, in tented bath-couches, washed by sprays, were two Tlixix.

The Gamintes pushed their prisoners forward. A sharp, salty, seaweed smell wafted from the lobster-creatures, a smell from Tenacity's remote past, seeming to bring with it images of tidal pools, of surf, of tangy breezes and scudding foam. The tents parted. The Tlixix reared above them.

Feelers quivering, antlers waving in agitation, massive crustacean heads bent in inspection, their faces, if such they could be called, alive with whiskery motion, and framed by the helmet-like upper segments of their body shells, which glistened green and blue.

For all their alienness there was a cold sense of power about the beasts. It was a feeling Krabbe had expected, and one which he relished.

A voice hoarse and breathless, harsh and clicking came from one of the Tlixix. In reply a Gaminte embarked on a long explanation in guttural tones. Then the Tlixix turned to the Earthmen and spoke again. Bouche raised his hands in a conciliatory gesture.

"We are strangers, Market Master," he answered in Terra standard. "We cannot understand you."

There was silence. All the Tenaciteans present, humanoid and crustacean, seemed mystified. It occurred to Krabbe that they might not have such a concept as a foreign language. The Tlixix had imposed their own on the dehydrate species as they evolved.

Behind him the door irised again. Through it poured more Gamintes, this time carrying everything that had been in Krabbe and Bouche's lodging: water drums, food packs, assorted items including weapons. All this was dumped in front of the Tlixix, who peered at it with their blank, white eyes.

A Gaminte picked up a water drum and shook it. Water sloshed inside.

As he put it down again Bouche bent to the goods. He had spotted the ear and throat translators. Suspiciously the guards lifted their flingers, aiming flenching blades as he handed one set to Krabbe and fitted the other to himself.

The Market Master's words were now intelligible. *"You are in possession of water! All water belongs to the Tlixix! How did you come by it?"*

His voice was like the roaring of surf. To fasten on the neckbands, the Earthmen had thrown back the hoods of their burnouses. The Tlixix became still, regarding them intently, as if puzzled.

"What is your tribe? From what part of the world do you come?"

Krabbe spoke, again experiencing the weird sensation of having his words whipped away to emerge from the voice-disk in an alien tongue.

"Our tribe does not exist in this world, Market Master. The water is ours, and nowhere in all the deserts will you find another people like us. We come from the stars."

The two Tlixix stared at one another then back at Krabbe.

"From the stars? What nonsense is this?"

"We can prove it. We come from the stars, and we are here to trade."

"And how did you come from the stars?"

Krabbe grinned. Incredulous though the lobsters were of what, after all, must seem a preposterous story, they would soon change their minds when they saw evidence of the technology the firm of Krabbe & Bouche had available.

"We came in a vehicle that is closed up like a barrel, or like this building. It carries its own air, for there is no air in between the stars. It now waits for us in the sky, too high to be seen."

"Do not waste our time with your ridiculous stories. What is the name of your tribe? Where did you get this water?"

"We can prove what we say, Market Master. If you will allow me to use a device among our goods, I will speak to our comrades aboard the vessel in the sky, and you will hear their voices."

"*Hear their voices?*"

"Yes, Market Master."

There was a pause. "Proceed."

Krabbe found the communicator and, again under the nervous gaze of flinger-wielding Gamintes, opened up its dish antenna.

Bouche took off his translator. "Here, you'd better let me do that." He took the handset from Krabbe and touched a tab.

"Are you there, O'Rourke? Come in, please."

Their most trusted bondman answered almost immediately. "O'Rourke here, Partner Bouche."

"We have made contact, O'Rourke. I am demonstrating that we have friends in orbit. That is all."

"Understood, Partner Bouche."

"Out."

The Market Master's companion uttered an exclamation and jerked his body, sending drops of water shooting off him. "*That strange noise comes from a long distance?*"

"That's correct, Market Master," Krabbe said with satisfaction.

"*And it works, perhaps, by sending inaudible radiations? Something similar to light, except it cannot be seen?*"

"Well, yes," Krabbe said slowly, blinking. "That's a good description."

"*Then it is true. There is such a device!*"

The Market Master himself turned this way and that, stalks and feelers in a frenzy. "*Seize these two! They have come to the market as liars and thieves. They have stolen our water. They have stolen the invention of the Analane! What else have they stolen? Seize them!*"

With gruff cries the terrifying Gamintes rushed forward.

CHAPTER SEVEN

Hrityu and Kurwer, who had been wandering the market in a fruit-less search, pleading with anyone who would listen to their entreaties, went wild with joy and relief when a Gaminte came to tell them the radiator had been found.

Hurrying to the Pavilion of Audience, they met a strange scene. The Crome, their enemy, was present. But so were two humanoids they could not identify, strangers of a pale greenish-yellow colour who stood with heads bowed before the lordly Tlixix. Around them were scattered a number of objects whose purpose was not clear.

Rherrsherrsh, the majestic Market Master, waved something in a manipulatory stalk.

"Come closer, Analane. Take this."

Gingerly Hrityu reached up and accepted the object. He inspected it curiously. It was a flat, rectangular box, surprisingly light for its size, made of a substance that was neither glass nor metal. Coloured strips and tabs decorated its surface.

"Do you confirm that this is your missing property?" the Tlixix rasped.

Hrityu looked again at the box, puzzled. "Why, no, Market Master. This is not our radiator. Our machine is much larger. What this is, I cannot say."

A rustling sigh came from within the transparent tents.

"You have never seen it before?"

"Never, Market Master."

Rherrsherrsh pointed his snout at the pale-skinned ones. His white eyes glistened.

Boris Bouche licked his lips. "We spoke the truth, Market Master," he said. "We come from another world. Allow us to prove it with a demonstration of our alienness."

"Proceed."

Bouche stepped to one of the water drums and unscrewed the cap. Using a ladle clipped to the side of the container, he dipped into its cool contents.

"Water, Market Master. We need it to stay alive, just as you do."

He was, as a matter of fact, feeling thirsty. He gulped down the water, ending with a sigh of satisfaction.

The dehydrate humanoids stared in stunned amazement. Even the Tlixix waved to and fro in their consternation.

"To any but ourselves water is poison!"

Krabbe took the ladle from Bouche and also dipped, swallowing a mouthful, then replacing the screw cap. He turned to face the Tlixix.

"That is because yours is a dried-out world, Market Master. The worlds where we live have plenty of water. It's the basis of our form of life."

"Then you are as we are."

Krabbe grinned broadly. "That's it. We are just like you."

Rherrsherrsh's eyes became moist with excitement as he leaned towards the humans. "And do you come to our world to trade?"

"That's it again, Market Master. We do indeed come to trade."

*

In the dust of the concourse the Analane looked at one another in bewilderment. They had been ushered from the pavilion before the strangers could divulge their intentions any further, as had the lone Crome, but that scarcely interested them in their dismay.

"All is lost," Kurwer murmured dejectedly.

Hrityu squared his thin shoulders. "Do not say that! There is still hope."

The Crome eyed the two haughtily and stepped forward.

"The Tlixix appear to think the apparatus you boast of really exists," he said thoughtfully. "Perhaps it does, after all. I, however did not steal it."

"Not you?" Hrityu challenged heatedly. "Who but you could possibly have a motive!"

"To that I have no answer," shrugged the Crome. "For a moment there, I was afraid the Market Master would cancel the permission he has already given for our onslaught—"

"Already?" Kurwer gasped.

The Crome grinned mercilessly. "It seems that in the excitement you were not informed. Yes, already. We attack in thirty courses of the sun. You will recall that we entered a plea for your extermination. While that was not expressly approved, it was not forbidden either. That's good enough for us."

"The Tlixix almost never allow extermination! You would not dare! There would have to be a compelling reason!"

"Almost never?" taunted the Crome. "Well, let me see what examples come to mind. Were not the Sliss exterminated, not long ago?"

"They had shrunk to no more than a hundred in number! We Analane number thousands!"

"Yes, thousands who have been destroying the prickle-stalks on which alone the Crome can live!" The Crome's tone had turned from haughtiness to indignation. "In another few turns of the sun it would be *we* who are extinct! *There* is your compelling reason, Analane! Your vile mould will do nothing to sustain us!"

With those words he turned his back on them and strode off.

Hrityu found that he was shivering.

"Did you hear that?" Kurwer said in a low voice. "The prickle-stalk campaign must have been more successful than we thought. They are on the verge of starvation!"

"Our aim was to reduce their numbers, not to wipe them out completely," Hrityu pointed out mildly. "Their reaction is out of proportion."

A Gaminte approached and handed over the flingers taken from them when they entered the Pavilion of Audience. Disconsolately they walked down the concourse.

"What shall we do?" Kurwer said. "We cannot return home with such colossal failure on our consciences."

"We must continue to search for the radiator." Hrityu paused. "Who were the strangers in the pavilion? I have never seen their like before. Their equipment looked interesting."

"I do not understand what I saw there," Kurwer admitted. "It appeared to me that they were *swallowing water*. But that cannot be so."

"Their talk was strange. They spoke of coming from another world. How can there be another world?"

"No doubt they are liars, like the Crome."

A voice came from Kurwer's left. "*A word with you, please, Analane.*"

A humanoid had stepped into the concourse to accost them. They stared at him. His colour was green, but a lighter shade than that of the Crome. He was roughly the height of an Analane, and was just as slender, but his face had nothing of Analane softness. It was sharp, narrow-jawed, the eyes upward-slanting and silvery bright. The skin was mottled, reptilian fashion, even on the face. His headcrest was large, and was echoed by similar fanlike structures on his back.

His flinger was a flashy affair, ornamented with shining crystals.

"Perhaps I can be of help to you."

"You are an Artaxa," Hrityu murmured. They were a little-known tribe, not given to travel. He had seen one once before, long ago.

"Yes. And you seek a device you call a radiator."

"News of our loss has travelled."

"I knew of your machine earlier, before it disappeared." The Artaxa's eyes gleamed like polished metal. "I know a great deal."

"But how—?"

For answer, the Artaxa did something peculiar. His ears, which up to now had been ordinary-looking, reshaped themselves into funnels which he extended outward from his skull, directing them this way and that.

"We of the Artaxa have exceptionally acute hearing, and can eavesdrop on private conversations even from a long way off. I was present in the Pavilion of Warfare on the day you met the representative of the Toureen."

His ears flattened themselves again. "As I said, I can help you. But if we are to proceed further it must be on a basis of trust and confidence. Otherwise much harm will result."

"Do you know the whereabouts of our radiator?" Hrityu demanded.

The Artaxa nodded.

"Then it must have been you—"

"Please." The greenskin raised a hand. "If we are to talk, let it be somewhere more private. I suggest a ride into the desert."

Hrityu considered the proposal. If the Artaxa was planning treachery, it was hard to see what he would gain by it.

He glanced at Kurwer, then said, "We shall take our vehicle. Come. To the park."

*

The wheel machine went bucking and sliding over the dunes. Eventually the bright pavilion were out of sight.

Hrityu disengaged the inner and outer wheel and applied the brake. He and Kurwer turned to the Artaxa who sat in the back of the apartment. The other laid aside his flinger, in a gesture of peace.

"Allow me to give you my name. I am Karvass, of the Artaxa."

43

Hrityu thought the circumstances for name exchanging unusual, to say the least. His crest bristled."Do you ask for our names? Frankly I do not see the need."

The Artaxa's facial membranes dilated slightly. "As you wish. But remember, I did ask for trust—as I am trusting you, more than you realize."

Kurwer leaned close to his companion. "Let us take him at his word."

Hrityu was silent. Then he softened. "Very well. I am Hrityu, of the Analane."

"And I," echoed Kurwer, "am Kurwer, of the Analane."

"Good." The Artaxa relaxed. He nodded. "Yes, as you already have suspected, it as I who stole your radiator. I immediately recognised its value to my race, and I was determined to acquire it. At the same time, I had nothing of like value to offer in exchange."

"And therefore you simply took it?" Kurwer exploded. "This is outrageous! The Tlixix will punish your tribe severely!"

Hrityu waved him quiet. "So you have our machine," he said to the Artaxa coldly. "What is it you want with us?"

"I have examined the device. It appears to function as you claim—though without a partner I have not been able to test it thoroughly. It is the means by which it works that remains a mystery. I do not think our mechanics will be able to duplicate it. Therefore I need you."

"You want our cooperation? Offering nothing in return?" Hrityu said incredulously.

"Not quite. I have a proposal to put to you. Let me ask you a question. Since arriving here you have had dealings with the Tlixix. How would you describe their treatment of you?"

"We can hardly be pleased with someone who consents to our extermination!" Hrityu grumbled bitterly. "We have met with nothing but injustice!"

"That is what emboldens me to reveal myself to you," the Artaxa said. There was a grim satisfaction in his voice. "The Crome representative has been boasting everywhere of the edict he has obtained. What I propose is an alliance."

"An alliance?" Hrityu repeated in puzzlement. "Against the Crome?"

"Not just against the Crome. Against the Tlixix!"

Both Analane stared at him in shock.

Karvass continued calmly: "Let me tell you something of my race. You know little, for we Artaxa are secretive. Most believe us to be few in number, and we encourage this belief. In fact, our tribe has increased to a size unprecedented since the Great Dehydration. There are nearly one hundred thousand of us. Not even the Tlixix know this."

Kurwer shook his head. "How could such a huge tribe stay hidden from the Tlixix? They know everything."

"We have had the help of the Sawune, the lizard race who live underground. They led us to vast underground caverns which we have made our home, and there we have worked and planned. Our hope is to come out into the sun and there build giant camps where we may live. Before the world changed the Tlixix built such great camps. All are buried by sand now."

The Analane had heard tales of the stupendous habitations of the Tlixix in olden days.

Karvass went on: "The Tlixix, naturally, would never allow this. If they even learned of our great numbers they would promote wars of extermination against us, for they maintain their power by keeping tribes small and in constant warfare with one another. Yet why should the Tlixix dominate the world? They belong to the far past, before the great change. They must huddle in their hydroriums, and scheme to keep us pitted against one another. Yet rightly, the world belongs to us. Do you understand me, Analane?"

"But how can you think to challenge the Tlixix?" Kurwer asked in a hushed tone.

"We *shall* challenge them. We shall challenge them *by making war on them*. The Artaxa, the Sawune and such tribes as will join forces with us will fight whoever chooses to defend them. The Tlixix will be swept away."

"What will become of them?" Hrityu said in awe.

"No doubt they will all perish. Life is virtually impossible for them unless they make use of creatures like ourselves. They are not made for this world."

In stony silence the Analane sat contemplating the almost unbelievable thoughts that had just been put to them. A world without the Market Masters was hard to envisage.

"Then this is the alliance you offer," Hrityu said.

"Yes. I stole your radiator to put it into our hands rather than in the pincers of the Tlixix. Think what it will mean if tribe can speak to tribe, camp to camp, across the world! We shall be able to outflank our enemies and stall their every move. And now there is every reason for the whole tribe of the Analane to join us. The Tlixix are not your friends. This is the best way you can save yourselves."

"Is it?" Hrityu questioned stiffly. "We could, if we wished, go to the Tlixix and inform them of your plans. If we recover the radiator then . . . "

The Artaxa chuckled. "You could kill me here and now if you chose. I told you I was putting my trust in you. In neither case, however, would you be likely to regain the radiator, and so would not be able to obtain the eruptionite with which you thought to defend your tribe."

The Analane started at the mention of the secret weapon. Karvass chuckled again. "You would not obtain the eruptionite in any case. I have talked with Nussmussa of the Toureen. He has gone to consult the elders of his tribe, and it is close to certain that they will opt to join the alliance. I am confident that you will do the same. We shall have eruptionite! We shall have radiators! We shall be invincible!"

"But when is this uprising to take place?" Kurwer wanted to know. "What if the Crome attack first?"

"If you ally yourselves with our cause, we shall help you. Artaxa will fight alongside Analane, and our numbers alone ensure that you cannot be defeated by the Crome."

Hrityu pondered. "Only the elders of the Analane can make this decision."

"They will be guided by your advice."

"And yet respect for the Tlixix is a tradition hard to break."

"Even when one's tribe faces extinction? I think not. And when they realize that without the Tlixix an age of progress dawns upon the world . . . "

"He is right!" Kurwer exclaimed suddenly. "This is the only real option open to us, Hrityu! We owe the Tlixix nothing!"

"I agree," Hrityu said slowly. "We owe them nothing." He turned to Karvass. "I suggest you now lead us to where you have hidden our radiator."

"It is already within your view. Drive to that rock over there."

Karvass pointed to an outcrop midway to the horizon. Hrityu obeyed him, but it was not until he had halted the vehicle that he saw that the rock was not a rock at all but a sheet of grey, fibrous cloth stretched over something bulky, its edges weighed down with sand. It was a cunning disguise. Karvass jumped to the ground and cumbersomely removed the cloth. Revealed was a narrow, smooth vehicle with a bow-like prow and a passenger compartment protected by a raked glass windscreen.

The two Analane followed him and saw, nestling side by side under the windscreen, their radiator and receiver. Their facial membranes quivered.

"This is my plan," Karvass said briskly. "Firstly, I will take you to our secret camp. There a force will be assembled to aid in your fight against the Crome, and one of you can return home with it. The other will remain to teach us the secrets of your device."

The Artaxa's bright silver eyes stared at them. "What is your answer? I have thrown myself on your mercy. You are two against one. There is nothing to prevent you from killing me here and now and taking back your property. But I do not believe you will be so foolish. Instead, let us be comrades-in-arms!"

Karvass stepped forward, metal accoutrements clinking. He clasped Hrityu by the wrist in the worldwide gesture of trust and agreement.

And Hrityu clasped the green-skinned humanoid by his other wrist, completing the sign.

"Very well, then! Full speed to the camp of the Artaxa!"

CHAPTER EIGHT

The hydrorium towards which the desert caravan hummed was, according to the Gaminte guards, the largest on the planet. It hove into view like a dome-shaped mountain, the metal exterior scored to dullness by centuries of wind-blown sand.

Boris Bouche judged the curve of the dome to be a cycloid, a shape much used by human engineers. It impressed him that the Tlixix could construct a cycloid on this scale. He scanned the terrain where the dome stood. It had been built on the edge of an escarpment, beneath which a level plain stretched to the horizon. Clearly this had been a shoreline, in the days before all ocean water disappeared into Tenacity's interior.

They were in the foremost of four large desert drays. The journey from the World Market had taken a tiresome two Earth days. A suggestion that transport be left to one of the *Enterprise's* lighters had met with a curt refusal on the part of the Tlixix, who continued to treat the Earthmen as prisoners, albeit honoured ones. They still retained all of Krabbe and Bouche's equipment, except for the translator sets.

They didn't know, of course, that the *Enterprise* was watching the progress or the caravan through the interferometric telescope.

The partners lounged on the foredeck, protected by a glass canopy, in company with three Gamintes. Market Master Rherrsherrsh was semi-submerged in a spray-bath in the rear, separated from them by a partition. His colleague at the World Market had gone ahead in a fast vehicle to brief the Tlixix ruling council. Behind them, in the second dray, was Krabbe and Bouche's supply of food and water.

The powerful radium motor hummed as the Gaminte driver headed the dray towards the dome's tunnel entrance. Bouche scowled, rubbing his jaw. Krabbe, by contrast, smiled happily. He had noticed how his partner got tense at these moments. He, however, was convinced that everything was going well. Sure, the lobsters were going to have an incredulity problem. The tale they were being told was scarcely believable, from their point of view.

But Krabbe had dealt with a range of alien races, and he had come up with a common denominator. It didn't matter what an intelligent species looked like, or what strange habits and outlooks it had. There was a common touchstone for the whole galaxy, probably for the whole universe, which made it possible to do business.

Greed and self-interest.

The Gamintes were hurriedly donning skintight suits complete with facemasks. They were preparing themselves for the conditions inside the dome. If naked they could not tolerate a water-rich environment for very long. The tunnel turned out to be a multi-stage vapour lock. One by one doors opened in sequence. Then the sixth door opened, they trundled into the hydrorium.

The scene was stunning.

They saw what appeared to be a rocky shoreline, full of creeks and beaches, fringing a calm ocean. There was little sense of being in an enclosed space, and even less of being on the planet as they had experienced it so far. The dome's roof was coloured blue—a softer blue than the sharp azure which bedecked present-day Tenacity—and gave the impression of a sky extending to a distant horizon. Lounging and splashing in the water were hundreds of Tlixix.

The lobster creatures had managed to preserve a fragment of their former world. Several fragments, rather. This was one of several such refuges.

Krabbe was awe-struck. "What a place!"

Bouche nodded. As the Gamintes slid back the desert rover's transparent canopy a refreshing sea-smell wafted in, carried by a distinct breeze. That would be part of the artificial environment's circulation system, Bouche thought to himself.

"This is probably only part of it," he said to Krabbe. "See those openings in the rocks? My guess is they lead to excavations underground."

"Yes. What we're looking at is a pleasure area."

"Well, a little more then that. It's also a psychological necessity. The lobsters need to have something of the environment they evolved in."

The masked Gamintes swung a ramp over the side of the desert dray, then picked up their flingers. The curtain screening the rear compartment swished aside. Market Master Rherrsherrsh came through, moving on crab-like legs, stalks and antlers waving. An unmistakable seaweed smell wafted from him as he swept by them and proceeded down the ramp.

The Gamintes motioned the Earthmen to follow. They crossed a sandy beach. An odd sensation assailed Krabbe. To see more-than-people-sized lobster-like creatures disporting by a seaside made the scene surreal, as if invented by a mad artist. He could almost expect to find shrimp-sized humans lurking beneath rocks in the pools.

As Bouche had surmised, they were making for one of the cave entrances. Inside, the tunnel angled sharply down, lit by radium lamps and forking frequently.

"Did you notice something back there?" Bouche asked.

"What?"

"The lobsters on the beach. Did you see any *little* lobsters? Or larval forms or anything? Everybody was full grown."

"Maybe the young are kept in nurseries. They probably hatch from eggs."

"Yes, or maybe there just aren't many of them. A low birthrate would make sense in these conditions. And a low birthrate suggests a long-living species. These guys are probably *old*. And their leaders will be oldest of all."

"I see what you mean," nodded Krabbe. He and his partner had learned to gauge the shrewdness of a species by the length of its life-cycle. They had once struck a deal on a planet where individuals lived for no more than two Earth years. It had been like taking candy from a child.

Here they were going to have their work cut out. From the look of it Tlixix individuals lived a long time. They would have to, to gain the experience and deviousness needed to keep control of Tenacity.

They continued downward for some time, until the tunnel widened into a globe-shaped chamber. Their path was here blocked by four Tlixix who carried in their pincers versions of the weapon also toted by the Gamintes and which seemed to be almost universal on Tenacity: a kind of catapult-crossbow flinging a whirling curved blade.

In a sense the newcomers answered Bouche's question. They were smaller than the Tlixix Krabbe and Bouche had seen so far, which probably meant that they were younger. Their sheen was different, greener, and a fresher smell came from them.

One spoke to Rherrsherrsh, who turned to face the party behind him. The partners switched their translators on.

"The Gamintes may leave the refuge."

Thankfully the black guards turned and retreated.

Bouche turned his translator off again. "See that? Now we can be sure they're taking us seriously. The Gamintes are the lobster's guard dogs. It wouldn't do to let them get wind of what's coming."

That's right, Krabbe thought. But two more points clicked up in his mind. One, the Tlixix were capable of fielding fighting troops of their own. And two, the partners were still under guard.

It might become necessary to let the Tlixix know, accidentally as it were, that their movements had been followed by their colleagues in space. And that the *Enterprise* could smash this dome like an egg.

At the other end of the chamber a door irised open.

Flanked by the Tlixix guards, the Earthmen went through. They now stood in a much larger chamber utterly drenched in a fine drizzle. The floor was awash. And in the centre lay a spacious pool where half a dozen Tlixix lolled.

An air of luxury pervaded the chamber, which was bathed in golden light. The walls were pale blue, like the roof of the larger dome. A sea-weed-like plant of various reddish hues floated in the pool end trailed across the floor in long ribbons, giving off a pungent smell.

Rherrsherrsh beckoned Krabbe and Bouche to come forward. Their burnooses already soaked, the Earthman approached the pool, throwing back their cowls to reveal their faces as three Tlixix reared up from the water to scrutinise them.

There was a marked difference between the creatures in the pool and Rherrsherrsh and his companion in the World Market. Whereas Rherrsherrsh's face was generally agitated, his whiskers constantly twitching, the crustacean faces now confronting them possessed an icy stillness. These creatures were larger, too, and the greenish-blue of their segmented body-shells tended to yellow. A feeling of hoariness sur-rounded them.

They were quite possibly several centuries old.

A voice like a soft roar came from the middle one of the three.

"So you claim to come from another world in space."

"Yes," Krabbe replied.

"And you claim you can give our world back its water."

"Yes."

"Then you must tell us how."

Krabbe let his partner answer that.

"First of all," Bouche said dryly, "where do you think your water went to when it disappeared?"

The Tlixix leader paused, and spoke less vociferously.

"We do not know. Some say it evaporated into space, others that it sank into the sand. In past times our engineers dug deep wells. But no water was ever found."

"The principle was right. The water went into the ground. But it went a long way down, much further than you could ever reach by digging. Now, our arts are superior to yours. We can bring the water back."

"You still do not say how."

"We have ways of forcing the water back up to the surface. It will form oceans once more. There will be rain."

"What if it drains away again?"

"We can stop that happening."

"How do you force the water back up?"

"That is difficult to explain. Essentially, we reverse the process that caused it to drain away. If you wish, you can talk to our engineers about it."

The Tlixix who had been speaking broke off and splashed into the pool. All six of the beasts began surging about in the water as if in great excitement. This must be absolutely incredible to them, Krabbe thought. They scarcely know what to make of it.

At length the sloshing water subsided. The Tlixix leader reared over them again.

"How do we know you are what you say? How do we know you are not a mutated species of our own world who have found a supply of water and learned to live on it? You will take one of us to this ship which you say hangs in space."

"Agreed."

The Tlixix turned his four milky eyes on the Earthmen, studying them. Power exuded from the creature. Power and a ruthless determination. "There is equipment with which to communicate with your ship?"

"Yes, that's right."

"All your property has been brought here. You will arrange for our representative to see the ship in space. Meantime, you remain here as our guests."

The Tlixix spoke with a finality which caused Krabbe to glance at the crustacean guards behind him.

Turning off his translator, Bouche spoke aside to him. "They don't trust us yet. They're measuring us by their own cloth. They probably suspect we aim to control them the same way they control the dehydrate species. But don't worry. We're offering them paradise. They're not going to be able to refuse."

He turned the translator back on as the master of Tenacity spoke again.

"And if you restore our world to us, what do you want in return?"

Krabbe and Bouche both sighed.

The negotiating was about to begin.

*

Planets a gogetter company could realistically expect to do business with were generally a patchwork of authorities—nations, empires or the like—and that made matters complicated. Sometimes a gogetter's intervention would spark off a destructive war, rendering any contract drawn up unenforceable.

To come upon a planet under one set of rules was a pretty good piece of luck. It meant the contract could be global.

However it was dressed up, what a gogetter wanted was to exchange beads for Manhattan. In return for some service or good-looking piece of technology, he would claim from the owner of a territory all interstellar trading rights, sewn together so as to hold up in a human court of law. If Krabbe and Bouche had their way, the lobsters' ownership of their world would ultimately consist of little more than their tenancy of it.

All off-world commerce, all mining, manufacturing and trading not of a purely domestic character would belong solely to the firm of Krabbe & Bouche, Partners. Exclusive rights in the uninhabited bodies of the local planetary system would also be thrown in.

Exclusivity was in fact what gave the contract its value as an asset. The gogetter would rarely take up the options himself. But when, sooner or later, one of the rapacious large corporations decided to make use of the find it would have to license the right to do so. Meantime, registering the contract increased Krabbe & Bouche's credit.

Bouche chuckled. "I wonder what these lobsters would think if they found out our licence to operate has been revoked," he said, translator off.

It probably would be hard to explain to them that actually it didn't make any difference. The contract drawn up and registered would still be valid.

That was one of many useful lacunae in the law.

CHAPTER NINE

"O'Rourke calling Castaneda."

Resting in the cool of the tent, Roncie answered, "Northrop here. Castaneda is at the site."

O'Rourke's voice became distinctly frosty as he recognised the would-be ship-jumper. "Tell Castaneda the partners are in a position to strike a deal. Is the surveying complete?"

"Just about."

Three teams had been hopping about the planet for the past few days, carrying out seismic tests. Eight catastrophe fracture zones had been mapped in detail. If they got the go-ahead, the teams could start drilling.

"The negotiating is to take place in the natives' main dome," O'Rourke went on. "The partners want Shelley present, and also Castaneda. The lobsters are asking for technical details. Got that?"

"Got it."

"I'm sending a lighter down. Meantime you can put the drilling rigs in place. No point wasting time."

"Right." Northrop hesitated. "One other thing. Did the partners beam up language translation?"

"What if they did?"

"Pass it on to us, will you?"

"What for?" Northrop asked suspiciously.

"We've spotted bands of dehydrate natives roaming around. We might need to talk to them."

There was an ominous pause before O'Rourke replied. "There's a security issue here. On no account must the dehydrate species gain any hint of what is being planned. Request denied."

"Do you think I'm an idiot? Tenacity dehydrates have a traditional warrior culture. They'll attack us if we can't talk to them."

"You are a bond jumper," O'Rourke said, with no attempt to hide his hostility. "Any request like that must come from Castaneda."

He cut the connection. Northrop turned as Castaneda entered the tent. The team leader's skin was a bright green in hue. He was wearing several layers of radpaint.

"The show's on," Northrop informed him, and relayed what O'Rourke had said about the negotiation and drilling. "By the way," he added, "could you ask him for the partners' translation package? He got sticky when I asked him for it. Seemed to think I'd blab to the dehydrates."

With a tired air Castaneda keyed the communicator and got O'Rourke back.

"Are the shock tubes assembled yet?" he asked him.

"They'll be ready when you need them," O'Rourke told him.

"Drawing up a legally binding agreement with the lobsters is going to take some time yet. The lighter is leaving now. You'll need a geological map of the faultline and also a map of the projected new ocean. The natives should be warned if they'll need to evacuate any of their refuges."

"I doubt if that will be necessary. The new ocean will lie on the bed of the old one."

Northrop nudged him. Castaneda grunted in bewilderment, then said, "Oh yes. We want the language package. Might need to talk to the locals if we're to continue operation down here."

"Are you sure of that?"

"Of course I'm sure," Castaneda said testily, "why do you think I'm asking?"

"All right. Get ready to cop."

After a warning bleep, the language translation package was dumped into the communicator's memory.

Castaneda rummaged about the tent. He found a scroll-screen with his charts stored on it. "Wonder if the lobsters have decent eyesight?" he wondered. "Bet I'm down to drawing maps in the sand."

"It'll be all right. Shelley has the harder job."

Castaneda snorted. "Have you never seen the partners in a negotiation? Shelley has practically nothing to do. Krabbe and Bouche will do nearly all the talking. Shelley's job is to make what comes out legally watertight. It's vital the lobsters can't claim they weren't party to the agreement if it comes to a fight in the courts."

Naturally Northrop was familiar with this aspect of a gogetter's fortunes. The laws dealing with contracts drawn up with aliens were extensive. Understandably, they leaned heavily in favour of the human party.

He followed Castaneda out of the tent. Tenacity's endlessly rolling dunes stretched in all directions. The sand was the colour of sulfur and would probably induce sand blindness if one were left in it for too long.

Some of the team had taken to wearing dark goggles, both for that reason and so the fine sand itself would not irritate their eyes.

The three others on the team were tinkering with the squat bulk of the drilling rig, which had the seismic detector beside it. The rig's energy beam would slice its way through ten kilometers of shale and basalt in only a few days, leaving a shaft wide enough to lower a shock tube down. The only problem would be if the shaft filled with water. Then the tube might have to be forced to its proper depth.

"I never heard of this ocean-draining phenomenon before," Northrop said. "Is it common?"

The geologist shook his head. "As far as I know it's unique. In my view it's a cusp event related to the exact magnitude of Tenacity's mass. Rock porosity is perfectly common, of course. It's caused by vulcanism. Volcanoes result from the melting of a planet's basaltic mantle. The melt is never uniform: it occurs at dihedral angles between rock crystals. The melt regions then join up to create a network, and in effect the rock becomes a sponge filled with molten material, which pressure forces to the surface and you have an eruption. Normally the sponge is then filled up with more mantle rock, acting elastically over long periods of time.

"What seems to have happened on Tenacity is that the interstices left by vulcanism were never filled up. If the planet had been only slightly smaller there would have been little vulcanism and so no giant porous regions. Any larger and pressure from below would certainly have filled up the interstices, instead of leaving a layer of sponge ready to soak up all the surface water."

"So it all hangs on a fine balance, eh?"

Northrop had followed the explanation absent-mindedly. He glanced overhead. The lighter dispatched by O'Rourke was descending at reckless speed, optical distortion from its inertial field resembling heat haze. Like a thrown cushion, it plumped down on the yellow sand.

"See you, Roncie. Wish me luck."

"Sure."

Castaneda climbed into the lighter. Northrop watched it fling itself into the air and streak into the distance, swiftly disappearing.

A movement on the near horizon, in the direction of the small, bright sun, caught his attention. The terrain rose somewhat there, forming a low ridge. Northrop took out a magnifier and pointed the scope.

On the small screen, two vehicles were sliding down the ridge, piling sand in front of them. One was boat-like, lacking any wheels that he could see, and ploughed through the sand as though through water.

The other was larger, an ungainly contraption with big wheels which flashed as they revolved. Both craft seemed to be moving with haste, and the large one was having trouble negotiating the slope at such speed. Once, it nearly turned over.

Soon, Northrop saw the reason for such hurry. The vehicles were fleeing from pursuers which sought to cut them off, large flat hovercraft—or so it seemed—which blew up sand around their edges. Three of them soared over the ridge.

All five vehicles were heading this way.

*

For day after day Hrityu and Kurwer had followed their Artaxan ally across the desert. The Artaxan camp, he promisedthem, was now not far off.

It was as the sun was descending on the third day that the blowcraft found then. In them were both Crome and Gamintes—a combination of sinister import to the Analane.

Karvass immediately turned his vehicle aside, followed by the Analane. They were attempting to lose themselves among the dunes before being spotted. The hope was futile: the three blowcraft came surging over the sand in pursuit. The blowcraft, which travelled by lifting themselves off the ground by means of a blast of air, were little more than moving platforms surrounded by balustrades. They were packed with gesticulating, yelling warriors. A carelessly aimed flenching blade whirred over Hrityu's head. Kurwer grabbed his own flinger ready to retaliate, but it was clear the three travellers could not hold their own and would quickly be overwhelmed.

"Follow me!" Karvass called out.

Again he turned his vehicle and went coursing at full speed towards a long ridge in the middle distance. Hrityu placed his own vehicle's outer wheels on maximum gearing. Briefly they slid on the sand before the craft picked up speed. He could see what the Artaxan's strategy was. He was counting on the blowcraft being unable to mount the ridge, allowing time to make an escape.

This was one of their disadvantages. Otherwise blowcraft were favoured by raiders roaming the desert looking for prey, as on level ground they were capable of quick bursts of speed. The war whoops grew louder as the pursuers gained on their victims. By now Karvass had reached the foot of the ridge and the prow of his craft heaved itself on to the slope, hurtling straight up it with ease. The Analane were not far behind; but their own vehicle could not climb nearly as swiftly. Hrityu turned first left then right so that the big wheels could bite into the hillside, mounting zigzag fashion.

Atop the ridge he paused and looked down. All three blowcraft had launched themselves on to the slope. The curtains holding in the cushions of air on which they floated flapped and bulged with the effort. But after mounting so far, they all began to slide back down.

Kurwer laughed. "So much for them!"

His glee was short-lived. Once again the blowcraft attempted the slope, adopting a zigzag tactic of their own and attacking the hillside slantwise. Slowly, slipping as rotating, the occupants hanging on to the balustrades, they were approaching the summit.

Hrityu hastily put the wheelcraft in motion again, hurtling down the other side of the ridge and nearly overturning in his hurry. Suddenly Kurwer pointed.

"Look!"

As he struggled to control the wheelcraft Hrityu glanced sidelong in the direction Kurwer indicated. Not too far off, there was a camp of some sort. There were pavilions—though only small ones—and what looked like big machines.

Only the Tlixix erected pavilions, but they were very big ones, and anyway it was inconceivable to find Tlixix out here in the wilderness. The machines, too, were unfamiliar.

Nevertheless the unknown camp presented an opportunity which the quick-thinking Karvass immediately seized. He made for the camp, followed by the Analane. Depending on whoever was in the camp, they might find allies or at least disconcert their pursuers.

On the other hand, Hrityu admitted to himself, the camp might contain yet more enemies.

Once having heaved themselves over the ridge the blowcraft slid down it with alacrity and shot across the desert, fanning out.

On the edge of the strange camp, the two fleeing craft found themselves caught in a deadly triangle.

All five vehicles now came to a stop. Gamintes and Crome clambered from their craft. They stood waving their flingers, jeering and laughing.

"We are lost," Kurwer muttered. "What aid will there be for our tribe now?"

Hrityu took time to notice the inhabitants of the camp. They were humanoid, but their bodies were clad in material of some kind. They were pale green in colour, and lacked head crests. Three stood by one or the big machines. Another had just emerged from one of the little pavilions.

Suddenly Hrityu realized where he had seen their like before—in the Pavilion of Audience, where members of a strange tribe had been accused of stealing the radiator.

And, incredibly, had swallowed water.

A Crome voice floated across the air. "Ho, Analane! Do you see our Gaminte brothers with us? They know that we have requested a war of extermination, and say the Tlixix are certain to agree. They are here to join us in the sport. We allow you the honour of being the first to face death!"

"So that is why the Gamintes are travelling with our enemies," Hrityu said grimly to his friend. "The Tlixix want us out of the way quickly. I wonder why?"

"It was ever their way," Kurwer replied dolefully. "They see some advantage in cultivating the Crome. Perhaps they wish to use them as they use the Gamintes."

"Let us hope they all perish together when the Artaxan alliance strike!"

Hrityu picked up his flinger.They stepped down from the wheelcraft and crouched beside it for what cover it gave. Flenching blades clanged against the side of the vehicle. Uttering ululating cries, a group of Crome charged.

Suddenly Kurwer sprang to his feet, head-crest rigid with anger.

"Come, Hrityu! Let us not die like lizards in a hole!"

He ran from cover, directly at the Crome. "Crome filth! You have eaten your last prickle stalk!"

A blade hurled itself from the shaft of his flinger. The group of Crome threw themselves to the ground, so that it whirred harmlessly above them and fell into the sand.

Before he could reload, one of the Crome had raised himself, taken aim and released his own blade.

And the aim was true.

*

On seeing the landcraft coming towards him, Northrop ducked back into the tent to get the two essentials when meeting aliens for the first time: a means of communication, and a weapon. He thrust a DE beamer in his belt, then spent a few seconds dumping the language conversion into an interpreter set, fastening it round his neck and putting the plugs in his ears.

Outside, the drama was developing. The hovercraft had surrounded their prey and come to a stop on the edge of the camp, appearing to ignore its existence. Two types of dehydrate were clambering from them, waving weapons and shouting insults.

One type was coal black and bore wiry silver hair. The other was quite different: a vivid green, with exaggeratedly wide shoulders, and several crests sweeping over their skulls.

Nervously the bondmen at the drilling rig were watching events, staying close to its bulk. Northrop turned his attention to the other two vehicles, those which were boxed in. The occupant of the boat-like craft was also green, but a much lighter hue. Once again a different species, he thought. From the wheeled vehicle two slight humanoids descended and crouched beside it for cover. They were an almost glowing blue. A memory stirred in Northrop's mind. He had watched observations made through the interferometric telescope, and on them he had seen an identical wheeled vehicle with two blue dehydrates. It had been in the parking lot of the world market run by the lobster creatures. The vehicle was quite striking: it had inner wheels which continued to turn even when the craft was stationary. This could, supposed, be the same vehicle and the same two humanoids.

That most fleeting, most distant of acquaintanceships was perhaps what irrationally influenced Northrop's next act. The impending fight was hopelessly one-sided. The three defenders stood little chance. All the warriors carried some or other version of the standard weapon on Tenacity—a sort of spring-loaded gun which shot rotating blades. He saw two or three of these go shimmering towards the wheeled vehicle, clanging against its side.

A group of greenskins charged.

Suddenly one of the blueskins leaped from the cover of the vehicle with a shout of defiance. He projected a blade, but this flew over the heads of the attackers as they threw themselves to the ground.

A greenskin then raised himself and let fly with a return shot. The shining golden metal of the blade flashed in the sunlight as it hurled itself towards its mark.

So it was that Northrop was able to see the effect of a flenching blade. Its cunning law in its curvature, which caused it to twist and turn within its target, and also to slide against bone, slicing the flesh from it. Gelatinous gobbets, a sickly green in colour, flew in all directions as it tore into the body of the blue dehydrate, seeming to strip him to the skeleton.

What remained toppled to the sand. The second blue dehydrate leaped to his feet with a cry of grief.

It was then that Northrop, without really thinking about it, drew the DE beamer from his belt and began firing. He took out the greenskin whose whirling blade had done such terrible work. Then he put the beamer on continuous and sent a swathe of death among the black and green warriors who had piled out of the hovercraft.

He stepped behind the tent as flenching blades whirred towards him. He heard them skirling against its metal skin. He circled the tent and began firing from the other side, targeting each hovercraft in turn.

Abruptly he held his fire. Sand was blowing up around the skirts of the vehicles. The hovercraft swayed, rotated and surged away, black and green warriors running after them to clamber aboard as best they could.

They were quickly out of sight. Northrop emerged from behind the tent and walked towards where the surviving blue dehydrate was standing over the butchered body of his companion.

"*Kurwer! My friend! My friend!*"

The slim humanoid turned as Roncie approached.

Hrityu, of the Analane, and Roncie Reaul Northrop, bondman of the firm of Krabbe & Bouche, stared at one another.

CHAPTER TEN

"Why did you help us, stranger?"

Northrop smiled lopsidedly. "I guess I have a natural sympathy with the losing side."

Hrityu stared unmoving. Northrop realized he had probably said something incomprehensible in Tenacity culture.

Now that the fight was over he was shaken by the carnage he had caused. A dozen bodies which had fallen to his DE beamer were tumbled on the sand. The weapon killed by administering an all-body shock lethal to almost any type of organism. For that reason it was the standard weapon used on aliens whose physical properties were unknown.

It could also be set on a wider angle, though in that case its dreadful efficacy was reduced. Northrop wondered what a narrowbeam or bullet would do to a dehydrate. Probably pass right through with little damage, unless it chanced to break a bone. In that sense, he admitted, the DE beamer was similar in principle to the whirling blades thrown by the native flingers.

Except that it wasn't nearly as messy.

Overcoming his puzzlement, Hrityu stepped to Northrop and offered his wrist. "I owe you my life. I am Hrityu, of the Analane."

"I'm sorry I couldn't save your friend."

Hrityu continued to stand with his wrist proffered. "I am Hrityu of the Analane," he repeated.

Northrop realized he had encountered a social ritual. He extended his own hand and felt dry, blue skin grasp his wrist. He grasped the others wrist in return.

"I am Roncie, er, of the Earthmen."

The Analane released his wrist and stepped back in surprise. "Earthmen? Your tribe lives underground, like the Sawune?"

"Er, number Well, sometimes."

The green dehydrate in the boat-like vehicle came walking towards them. Northrop noted his large head-crest and the fan-like growth running down his back.

He cast quick glances over him, the Analane, and the dead bodies strewn on the sand. Four distinct species were represented, but there were definite similarities among them. All were naked except for metal ornaments in the form of bangles and medallions. When a Tenacity dehydrate walked abroad it seemed he needed nothing but metal adornments and his weapons.

While in the brig Northrop had dipped extensively into Karl Krabbe's private library. It turned out that Krabbe was an *aficionado* of pre-spaceflight writer Edgar Rice Burroughs, who had written colourful adventure stories set on the planet Mars. Burroughs' Mars—or Barsoom, as its fictional inhabitants called it—had also been the stage for a warrior culture where men of different races carried nothing but weapons and ornaments. The comparison struck Northrop forcibly.

Karvass slowed his approach, distrustful of this strange being. In place of a head crest his pate was covered with a moss-like growth. He did not know what to make of it. Hrityu strove to reassure him, beckoning him closer and prevailing on him to extend his wrist.

"I am Karvass of the Artaxa."

"Er, I am Roncie of the Earthmen."

Karvass's facial membranes wrinkled in puzzlement at this, but Hrityu said nothing. Roncie spoke again.

"Do you wish to bury your friend's body?" he asked politely.

"Bury?" This time Hrityu was puzzled. "A Gaminte patrol will collect all the bodies eventually. Their sniffer animals can smell corpses from fifty langs."

Of course, Northrop thought. Corpses were valuable biological material. They might even contain traces of water.

It was hot standing under Tenacity's small bright sun. Northrop invited the dehydrates into his tent. They were reluctant to enter, associating such structures with the pavilions of the Tlixix, but at length, staring about them in wonderment at the furnishings and communicator equipment, they sat with him and talked.

Once within the tent, the first thing Northrop noticed about his guests was the absence of any smell. Alien creatures usually gave off an odour of some kind. The dryness of the atmosphere, and their peculiar physiology, was responsible, he decided.

They were guarded when he asked them why they were being hunted. He, of course, did not know that the black Gamintes were a police force acting for the Tlixix, the masters of the planet.

"Why did you help us?" Hrityu responded, repeating his earlier question. "Do you not fear the retribution of the Tlixix?"

"The Tlixix?" Northrop laughed at the mention of the lobsters, though he did not know how the translator would render a laughing noise. "No, I don't fear them. They don't rule my kind."

Hrityu and Karvass looked at one another in astonishment. Hrityu's bewilderment increased. He recalled again the strange scene in the Pavilion of Audience.

Could it be that these green men with moss for head crests were also in revolt against the Tlixix? Or—extraordinary thought!—could they hail from the ancient time of the Tlixix themselves, in view of their tolerance of water?

He didn't know what the truth was, but the stranger's words brought out anew the indignation he felt. "The green enemies you saw belong to the tribe of the Crome," he said in a rush, "and they have announced a war of extermination against my tribe, the Analane, a war to which the Tlixix have given consent! It is on a mission to save our tribe that I and my dear friend Kurwer were travelling, in company with Karvass of the Artaxa, who has promised us help."

The list of names and tribes came at Northrop in a barely intelligible babble. Such a patchwork of wars and quarrels was to be expected he supposed.

"If the Tlixix are against you, your position is dire," he commented.

Karvass's membranes were dilating in alarm as Hrityu appeared to be exposing the secret of the gathering alliance, but the Analane would not be stopped. "Not any more! The tyranny of the Tlixix will come to an end! We shall survive!"

Not knowing anything of local politics, Northrop received this announcement without surprise. A feeling of pity for the dehydrates assailed him, mingled with an undercurrent of guilt. The struggles of the desert tribes did not matter. The dehydrates would probably all perish when water came back to Tenacity.

He felt almost tempted to reveal what was going to happen, and maybe provoke the dehydrates into a general revolt in an attempt to prevent it. But he did not dare to do that. Krabbe and Bouche would have the legal right to kill him.

Suddenly Hrityu and Karvass became fidgety and uncomfortable. Northrop could guess why. The water vapour given off by his body was affecting them.

He rose, opened the flap of the tent, and gestured to the outside.

Thankfully the dehydrates followed his suggestion, though they had no real idea what was causing them discomfort.

Northrop hesitated. He glanced over to the men at the drilling rig. They were not looking his way. He retreated to the other side of the tent so that they could not see him.

"I hope you manage the rest of your journey without being attacked again," he said. "If not—perhaps this will help."

He knew he was being far too impulsive, but he took out the DE beamer and showed it to Hrityu. "This is the weapon I used on your enemies. All you do is aim this square part here, and press this stud." He demonstrated, flexing his finger without taking it past the safety guard. "This ring here widens the angle so you can take out more warriors, but it's weaker then and doesn't always kill."

He pressed the gun into the astonished Analane's hands. "Hide it somewhere so my friends don't see I've given it to you. Good luck. Maybe it will help defend your tribe, too. There are just under two hundred shots left in it."

He didn't know whether the translator was conveying everything he was saying, but he waved the dehydrates away, anxious not to get himself in trouble. Slowly they walked to their vehicles and boarded them. Inner wheels began to revolve. The prow of the desert boat began to glide through the sand.

Without looking back, Hrityu and Karvass departed.

*

On being conducted into the giant hydrorium Castaneda was overcome by astonishment mixed with nervousness. It was impressive, *seriously* impressive, to see so grandiose an artificial environment on so arid and poverty-stricken a world. If human beings had built it, of course, it would be a routine piece of engineering. But the lobsters had kept this going in adverse circumstances for a very long time. He doubted if his own species would have been able to do that. Something would have gone wrong sooner or later, perhaps of a social character. The delicate balance of a closed biological system would have collapsed.

Yes, the lobsters. That was what frightened him. They were capable. But they had the partners in their grasp, and might not realize what a catastrophe it would be for them if they did Krabbe and Bouche any harm.

As usual, the partners had breezed in apparently oblivious of any danger to themselves. It was one of their many qualities which Castaneda admired. But he wished he didn't have to follow them into the spider's parlour.

Being in the presence of the lobsters was scary, too. For all their alienness they exuded a familiar air of menace—the menace of a master race accustomed to command. The partners would have had a tougher job being taken seriously, Boris Bouche commented, if it hadn't been for their trick of swallowing water. That had set them apart from the dehydrates.

Krabbe and Bouche greeted Castaneda cheerily, almost drunkenly, draping a translator band around his neck on the instant. Castaneda was given no time for mental adjustment. He launched himself into his presentation before Tlixix leaders and scientists who reared over him in their rank-smelling pool. Then the scientists questioned him closely and at length. They were the repositories of all the knowledge of their race. They had their own map of pre-dehydration Tenacity, and compared it in detail with the one Castaneda had drawn up. His description of the faultlines fascinated them. It was the first explanation they had ever heard of how Tenacity lost its water. They cast their four milky-white eyes on the locations of the proposed drilling. They grew more and more excited.

The translation package was elegant. Using some deft algorithm, it managed to give a representation of the lobsters' hoary character, giving them voices that mostly were hoarsely ferocious but sometimes condescendingly gentle—just the sort of tones masters would develop for dealing with their slaves.

It took hours, but in the end they seemed convinced. Krabbe and Bouche took over again, together with Shelley, the lawyer. The Tlixix scientists remained, but now it was mainly the top lobsters who did the talking.

This time it was Castaneda's turn to be fascinated. He always was, every time he had been present when the partners came to the crunch in a negotiation. Piece by piece, they were buying a planet.

But there was one more thing. The Tlixix still wanted to see the big ship in orbit. That was their guarantee that they weren't being conned. And, they made it clear, they did not want either Krabbe or Bouche personally to be their guide. The partners were to stay on Tenacity pending the outcome of the project.

And so, once Shelley had drawn up the final contract, Castaneda found himself lofting Enterprise-ward in the lighter, in company with the lawyer and a high-ranking Tlixix, filling the cabin with the tang of seaweed.

CHAPTER ELEVEN

No description by Karvass could have prepared Hrityu for the underground camp of the Artaxa.

They had travelled far from the World Market. Continuing to follow the Artaxa, whose prowed craft ploughed its way endlessly through the shifting sand, Hrityu had been almost disappointed not to encounter more Gaminte patrols—or even better, Crome warbands. He would have liked the chance to try out the weapon given him by the mysterious moss-headed stranger.

At length, a cluster of hills appeared in close formation, the sand having been blown off their peaks to reveal multi-hued ochre rock. Karvass steered his sand-boat on a winding course among them, losing himself to Hrityu's view several times, until entering a box canyon. Hrityu was puzzled that he should make for so obvious a dead end; until he noticed, at the far end, a shadow cast by a broad overhanging shelf of rock.

Straight into that shadow plunged the sand-boat. More cautiously, Hrityu followed, coming to a halt on finding himself at the top of a wide bank which sloped dawn into underground darkness.

Karvass's craft was already out of sight. Hrityu motivated his outer wheels again, setting off down the slope,

Soon he was in pitch blackness, carefully holding back his vehicle as it slid and slithered on loose shale. He did not know how far underground he was when a greenish glow appeared below him, slowly swelling into a steady, soft light. And then he was nearly at the bottom of the incline, looking down into a huge cavern.

And what a cavern! In the light streaming from radium lamps placed all round the curving walls, the roof was a great vault of massed down-jutting crystals of enormous size, many of them phosphorescing in response to the radiation and adding brilliant colours to the general illumination: purple, orange and ghostly yellow. On the floor of the cavern was as large a camp as any Hrityu had seen. Artaxa were present in large numbers, swirling in the ritual dances of their tribe, working at countless tasks, hammering at pieces of metal which, presumably, had been forged and smelted elsewhere, or shaping naturally occurring glass and crystal. Visible here and there were also the white sinuous forms of Sawune lizards. This was an odd sight. Hrityu had never witnessed close cooperation between humanoids and lizards before, leaving aside trade relations at the World Market.

That was not all. Also present were a number of black humanoids, lacking head crests. Toureen. Nussmussa must already have brought in his tribe as allies. Presumably they had brought the secret of eruptionite with them. Provided its ingredients were available close at hand, stocks of the violent mixture were no doubt already being built up.

Neither would it take Hrityu long to impart the secret of the long-distance radiators. Essentially the device was simple; one need only understand the principle of its working, and what kind of resonating crystals to use. There was no time now, of course, to arrange negotiations with the elders of the Analane. For all he knew the Crome might at this very moment be launching their final attack on his home territory! It was urgent that he persuade the Artaxa to mount an expeditionary force almost immediately.

As he took in the incredible sight he saw that the giant cavity was in fact only the first of a series. On either side were arched openings leading to similar caverns. A shiver went through him. This was as impressive as the World Market, if not more so! Almost as impressive as the giant hydroriums in which the Tlixix lived! (Though he had never seen these and knew them only by repute; Gaminte patrols kept all other dehydrate tribes well away.)

He could truly believe in what the Artaxa proposed. The days of the Tlixix were numbered!

True, the thought cost him unwelcome feelings. He had been raised to revere the Tlixix. They were part of the world, like the deserts and the hills. To betray them, even not to obey them, were unthinkable concepts.

Until, that was, the Tlixix themselves betrayed the Analane!

He descended to the floor of the cavern and climbed out of his vehicle. Karvass approached accompanied by an elderly, venerable-looking Artaxa. Hrityu went through the name-exchanging ceremony. Then, at Karvass's behest, pulled the cover off the pair of radiators.

Hrityu and Karvass spent some time trying to explain what the radiator could do. Finally, inspecting it at length with puzzled interest, the elder gestured his understanding.

"A remarkable invention, but where is its advantage to us?"

"It is not a weapon in itself," Karvass admitted. "But it will be invaluable for coordinating strategy."

The elder turned to Hrityu. "What is your price for the secret of this invention?"

"Assistance for my tribe, and immediately!" Hrityu said eagerly. "The Tlixix have given our enemies the Crome permission to effect our extermination, and this may in fact already be in process of commission!"

"Extermination?" the Artaxa repeated thoughtfully. "That is not a common policy, even for the Tlixix. "

"It may be that the Tlixix are recruiting the Crome for the same role as the Gamintes," Karvass put in. "We were attacked by a mixed force on our way here."

"All who join with the Tlixix are our enemies, all who join with us against the Tlixix are our friends," the Artaxan elder exclaimed. He then said to Hrityu, "Do you pledge your tribe in alliance with us?"

"Even though I am not an elder, I believe I can promise that every Analane will be with you," Hrityu said fervently. "If any survive!"

"Then our help is also pledged. How long will it take you to instruct our artisans in the manufacture and use of your device?"

"Not long—it *must* be done quickly, for I am determined to accompany your force and take part in the battle—with this!"

Hrityu pulled the beamer given him by 'Roncie' from his weapons belt, where it kept company with his three knives.

The elder stared at it with incomprehension.

Karvass spoke. He described the attack in the desert, and how a humanoid of an unknown type had come to their rescue, killing several of the attackers with the weapon Hrityu now possessed. He described, too, the tiny pavilion, and how uncomfortable they had been inside it, 'like being in the Pavilion of Audience.'

"I wish to see this for myself," the Artaxan elder pronounced. "Come with me."

They followed him through the throng to the side of the cavern. Guards standing at the entrance of a narrow passage stood aside, then trooped after them as they entered it and emerged into a chamber which, like the passage itself, had obviously been carved from the rock by hand.

Here was yet another strange sight. Gamintes, stripped of weapons, were chained to the walls. Their glowing red eyes turned to the newcomers. The radium lamp fitted in the roof gave their silvery hair a greenish glow.

To see the favoured police force of the Tlixix in such a situation was a shock in itself. The Gamintes' faces, too, showed their outrage that such a thing could happen to them, as well as their trepidation as to what their fate was to be. They were half starved, their bodies thin and wasted. That meant that they had been here for quite a long time. Energy-economical dehydrate bodies needed food only at infrequent intervals. Hrityu himself had eaten only once since leaving his home camp, although his wheeled vehicle carried plentiful supplies.

The elder issued clipped orders. The shackles were thrown off one of the Gamintes, who was pushed roughly into the centre of the chamber.

The Artaxan elder made a gesture. "Proceed. Kill the captive."

An unsettling thought came to Hrityu, put there by the unfamiliarity of events. What would the Tlixix do if they learned of this vast camp and of the plot being concocted there?

Why they would muster all the resources at their command to destroy it!

And what gratitude might they show to the tribe which informed them of such a threat?

No! Hrityu pushed the thought aside. Even if he could now warn the Tlixix, he could not rely on them. They had proved that were not to be trusted. The only hope of survival for the Analane lay with the Artaxa.

Slowly Hrityu lifted the weapon. Remembering the attack in the desert, his reluctance vanished. The Gamintes stared at him blankly, including the one offered him for target practice.

The weapon did not *look* like a weapon. It was not a flinger, and simply looked like an arbitrarily shaped object.

Hrityu strove to recall what the moss-headed humanoid had said. *Press this stud.*

He did so. Nothing visible issued from the square-nosed device, but the effect on the Gaminte was instantaneous.He recoiled, seemed to convulse, then fell to the floor of the chamber and was still.

Karvass stepped forward, knelt and examined him.

"He is dead."

"A flinger could have done as much," pointed out the elder skeptically.

"There is more," Hrityu said. "Stand aside, Karvass. Let us see if this works, too."

With the fingers of his free hand, he turned the ring Northrop had shown him. He pointed the beamer at the line of prisoners directly in front of him.

Only the Gaminte directly in line with the gun knew that he was doomed and glared his hatred. Those on either side failed to appreciate that their turn had also come. They hung their heads in shame at not being able to help their comrade and uttered keening noises.

Again Hrityu pressed the stud.

The beam encompassed five Gamintes, though unlike the first victim they took some moments to die. First they went rigid, shivered, then slumped in their chains. While the surviving Gamintes looked on with horror Karvass announced them all, on inspection, to be dead. The elder gestured and led the way from the chamber.

He spoke first to Karvass.

"You have acquitted yourself well, Karvass. You have provided us with three new inventions, as well as with alliances with two more tribes. Your praises will be shouted at the next mass convocation."

He spoke then to Hrityu. "You, too, have performed excellently for your tribe. Your praises too will be shouted, if we are in time to help save your people from extinction. By the way, could not your radiator tell us what the situation is at your camp?"

"Only if we are within a hundred langs."

"I see . . . Well, a hundred langs is certainly a useful distance."

"There is something else that you should know," Hrityu said, making up his mind to reveal everything. "Karvass has described to you the strangers who gave me my weapon. That there are of an unknown tribe is not perhaps so unusual, for there are many tribes, and for that matter few know of the Artaxa. But I have seen members of this tribe before—in the Pavilion of Audience at the World Market. They were talking with the Tlixix. And they were consuming *water*, just as the Tlixix do!"

"*Water*? Did you say *water*?"

"Yes, elder!"

The Artaxa paused for long thoughtful moments. "That is hard to believe, for water is a deadly poison to all humanoids. Who is there to back up your word? Did you see this, Karvass?"

"No, elder, I did not. But I believe the Analane."

The elder's voice fell to a mutter. "What can it mean? What can it mean?"

He seemed to be in a reverie. "There *is* a possibility. The Tlixix may have bred a new type of servant race more like themselves, even though humanoid. Perhaps they are beginning to doubt the loyalty of the Gamintes." He pondered further. "But then they would have to share their water with them . . . puzzling . . . "

Suddenly he seemed to come to life again. "There must be an immediate convocation. This is what will be proposed. Hrityu of the Analane, you will without delay instruct our artisans in the manufacture and use of your 'radiator'. Meanwhile a force will be assembled to speed to the aid of your tribe. Karvass, there is also a task for you. Lead a raiding force to the water-eating strangers. We need to know more about them. Capture one, and bring him back here!"

*

Though their pleasure was to slosh luxuriously in abundant water, Tlixix could also make their way on dry land—though preferably, of course, on spume-drenched land, being adapted for clambering over rocky shoreline. On a dozen stalk-like legs the visiting VIP dragged himself through the corridors of the *Enterprise*, blue-tinged chitin scraping on the floor, shelled head with its four white eyes turning this way and that.

The welcoming party consisted of O'Rourke, looking irritated as usual, Spencer the planetologist, and most of the engineering team that was assembling the shock tubes. The protocol, though a trifle perfunctory, was adequate enough, the eminent personage being treated with utmost deference—though Castaneda, the only one wearing a translation necklace, found himself being called on to act as interpreter. "You'll know how to talk to them," O'Rourke had muttered hurriedly. "You've had the experience."

So Castaneda did his best. He had been present at a number of such courtesy tours in the past, usually conducted by the partners in person. On one occasion he had asked whether planet-bound aliens might not go into shock on being taken into space. Krabbe had scowled, dismissing the point with a wave of his hand.

"Anybody that feeble won't do business anyway, Carlos. They'll clam up, go into fugue."

Castaneda took the Tlixix on a circuitous route through the starship, giving the maximum impression of its size, showing the propulsion section, the engineering departments including shock tube assembly—this he carefully explained—and finally finishing up on the navigation bridge. There he put Tenacity on the main screen. He knew the effect this would have. He had seen it before, more than once. It did not matter what the species; the astonishment was the same.

"That is our world?"

The voice of the Tlixix came through the translator as a breathless whisper.

"That's your world," Castaneda confirmed flatly. "The one we're going to transform for you."

The four milk-white eyes were fixed on the screen as though hypnotised. Castaneda could almost hear the creature's thoughts.

His was a deliberate ploy. The vision of one's home world as an object, rather than a limitless environment, with dark space all around it, made the idea that it could be altered much more believable.

Finally the Tlixix pulled himself out of his trance. "I will inform my colleagues that you speak the truth," he said hoarsely.

Smiling faintly, O'Rourke nodded when Castaneda relayed the words. He turned to his secretary who stood behind him.

"Tell them to start drilling," he murmured.

CHAPTER TWELVE

Roncie didn't hear them coming.

Like most hot deserts, Tenacity grew cold during the night. Roncie huddled in his tent, trying to sleep. A faint thrumming sound, like a rope vibrating in the wind, filtered through the camp. It was the sound made by the drilling rig, dipping down through the basaltic crust, its e-m beam constantly returning itself to the resonance frequencies of the rock crystals it met to pull them apart molecule by molecule. A mound, or giant snake, went winding out over the desert, made up of the dust and rubble being shuffled out of the hole.

The work was going well. The project was turning out to be an even easier job than had been anticipated. Castaneda's men had been able to determine that only eight strategically placed shock tubes would be sufficient to realign the fracture plates. Three drilling rigs had been delivered by engineering so far, with another on the way. This camp, site A, had already drilled five kilometers down. When it reached its planned depth of ten kilometers the rig would be moved out to do the same elsewhere.

Roncie had managed to fall into a doze when a stealthy opening of the tent flap woke him up. Starlight showed through the opening, outlining an indistinct figure.

He sat up, thinking it was one of the survey team. "Swanson?"

Reaching out, he turned on the light, and only then discovered that the figure at the tent flap was a greenskinned humanoid. It had silvery slanting eyes, and a large headcrest. As was typical of its kind, the humanoid was naked except for bangles on the arms and a metal circlet at the neck. Roncie would have raised the alarm by yelling at the top of his voice, but for the fact that the dehydrate was pointing a weapon at him. It had a dull grey stock—or so it appeared in the lamplight—and a spring-loaded mechanism for shooting the helical blade which featured so prominently at the front end. Having seen the way such a blade could scythe the flesh from a man's bones, Roncie froze.

Damn. He didn't even have his DE beamer. He had given it to the other dehydrate, the one called Hrityu.

The desert dehydrate had not yet discharged the blade, which gave

Roncie heart. He reasoned that verbal communication might well be an advantage. Slowly, with infinite caution, he allowed his fingers to search the bedside table until they touched the translator necklace.

Still moving slowly, with an attempt at apparent casualness, he draped it on him in time to hear the dehydrate speak.

"Greetings, Roncie of the Earthmen."

Now he remembered encountering this form of humanoid before. He strove to recall the name.

"You are . . . Karvass? Of the Artaxa?"

The membranes on the other's face underwent a peculiar writhing motion, possibly the equivalent of a nod. The tent flap admitted two more Artaxa who ranged themselves on either side of the first. They, too, carried flingers.

"You must come with us," Karvass said. "Our tribal elders have much to ask you."

Roncie sprang from his bed, standing in the insulated utility suit he used as sleeping wear because of the cold. "We are under the protection of the Tlixix—"

These words seemed to provoke the Artaxa, who took a step forward and used his free hand to seize Roncie by the arm. The Earthman was surprised at the wiry strength of his slim, smooth muscles. Karvass dragged him to the tent flap. At the same time another Artaxa was searching the tent. He opened the lid of the water cask and recoiled as the smell of water hit him. Hastily he closed the flask and threw it to the third Artaxa who caught it deftly.

Also on the bedside chest was Roncie's uneaten supper and his breakfast for next morning, in the form of trays of sandwiches in transparent wrappers. The Artaxa poked the preparation with a forefinger.

"It is the tribesman's food."

He tucked the trays under his arm and turned to go.

With the guide rail of a flinger digging into his ribs, Roncie could not resist being ushered outside. The camp was in darkness. The desert, sulfur-coloured by day, became a powdery alum under the massed stars. It came to Roncie that the visitors from those stars had taken local politics too much for granted. Assured of the power of the Tlixix—as well as of their own superior armament—they had posted neither guards nor warning devices.

It was time to regain his nerve. Roncie cried out at the top of his voice.

"*Swanson! Pettiford! Help me! I'm being kidnapped!*"

Too bad, he was still wearing the translator. His voice rang out in both languages across the camp. The Artaxa quickened their pace, bundling him along. They turned as lights came on and heads poked out of tents further off. There were shouts of alarm.

Flingers clanged, flenching blades whirred. One tore through a tent covering, but the Artaxa were not aiming properly. Roncie was hustled into the desert and flung to the floor of a sandboat face down. In seconds the vehicle was in motion. With a slithering sound it mounted the nearby dune, putting the camp out of sight, then went coursing away.

Roncie groaned. There was no vehicle in the camp in which to make pursuit.

He could only hope that O'Rourke would take the matter seriously enough to track him down and mount a rescue, or at the very least persuade the Tlixix to do so.

But there was no guarantee of that.

*

Hrityu had left his wheeled vehicle in the underground camp. He travelled now in a much larger Artaxa sandboat, holding thirty warriors.

Forty similar vehicles were ranged on either side in a wide echelon, sandscrews propelling them at top speed. Raising his head above the side of the boat, Hrityu was filled with excitement at the sight of the task force.

True, it bothered him a little that his new allies, the Artaxa, were green like the Crome, and not blue like the Analane. Colour was a special bonding in battle. When the fighting got furious would the Artaxa remember who were their friends and who their foe?

He hoped so. They were, after all, a light green, not the deep green of the Crome.

The great rolling dunes were left behind. They came among isolated hills between which blew a wind that rippled the yellow sand in complicated patterns. Here, too, were the first of the standing stones that marked the margins of Analane tribal territory. It alarmed Hrityu to see one of these tumbled on its side.

Before long the echelon of sandboats swept past a food mountain, on whose rocky side grew the blue-green mould necessary to Analane existence. Again he was alarmed. No Analane were to be seen. The mould crop was being left ungathered.

Worse, in the distance he saw lifeless bodies, relics of a recent fight.

The sandboats slowed to avoid the boulders which strewed the terrain hereabouts. Topping a rise, the riders beheld a great saucer-shaped depression.

It was the main camp of the Analane, and at present it was the scene of what could well have been their last battle.

There had clearly been a great slaughter, and the Analane were never numerous. The females and young were gathered at the centre of the amphitheatre. The surviving male warriors were arranged around them in a star formation. A horde of green Crome, a few black Gamintes among them, surrounded the star and mounted charge after charge, shrieking war-cries. Flenching blades flashed. Gobbets of flesh, sliced from the bone, flew in all directions as warriors fell and died on both sides.

Steadily the numbers of the Analane were diminishing.

Hrityu hugged to his chest the weapon given him by the 'Earthman'. The sight of his tribe being exterminated filled him with a greater rage than any he had known before.

He set the weapon's ring to full intensity. Better to leave one Crome dead than injure ten who might rise again!

The sandboats came to a halt poised over the lip of the depression. Twelve hundred warriors climbed out. The spectacle of the battle had aroused them. The Artaxa marshal raised his flinger and uttered a loud ululating cry, to be answered by a throbbing, "Hoohoohoohoo . . . "

The task force rushed shrieking down the slope.

*

Karl Krabbe took the news of Roncie Northrop's abduction with mild annoyance.

The report had come from O'Rourke. "A dehydrate raiding party, it seems."

Krabbe and Bouche were still in the great hydrorium, in an apartment given them by the Tlixix. 'Apartment' was perhaps the wrong word. The walls were made of a light metal glistening with condensation. Furnishings consisted of boulders from the artificial seashore to use as chairs. They smelled of seaweed.

The partners agreed it would be good to get back to the *Enterprise*.

"Have you been able to keep track of him?"

Testily, O'Rourke replied, "May I remind you, sir, that Northrop is of doubtful loyalty? That he has already tried to abscond once? Maybe we shouldn't worry too much about him."

"Please be in less of a hurry to divest us of useful personnel, O'Rourke," Krabbe drawled. "They're hard to come by out here. See if you can find him."

"Yes, sir." O'Rourke's voice was grumpy. "Though the trail will be cold by now. He was taken an hour ago. And the interferometric telescope isn't tuned to infrared, so we won't be able to start looking till the region rotates into daylight. Even then we would have to move the ship to do a proper job."

He ended the last on an interrogative note, as if encouraging Krabbe to tell him not to bother. After a pause, he added, "I take it this effort should not be allowed to delay the main activity in any way?"

"Well, of course, the project is the main thing." Krabbe yawned, resignedly aware that he had given O'Rourke the excuse he sought to do little or nothing to help Northrop. He was feeling tired. "You'd better tell Castaneda what's happened."

After O'Rourke had signed off he turned to Bouche, who was toying with his supper. "Why do you think those pesky desert-dwelling Barsoomians made off with our bondman? I thought the Tlixix had them well under control."

Bouche shrugged. "Maybe they want to see if he's any good to eat."

He conveyed a morsel of reddish crustacean flesh to his mouth. He did not appear to relish it.

For some perverse reason, he had got the *Enterprise* to send down a whole crateful of lobster thermidor.

CHAPTER THIRTEEN

By the time he reached the camp of the Artaxa Roncie Northrop was very hungry, very thirsty, and near the end of his tether. He had tried to eke out the water, but it became so hot during the day! The canteen had less than a pint left in it now.

As for the food, he had starved himself at first, but as the water steadily disappeared down his throat he began to wonder what the point of that might be. Thirst would kill him before starvation did. So he had allowed himself half a sandwich a day.

Except that yesterday he had eaten only one quarter of a sandwich. So he had a quarter left.

During daylight he continually scanned the sky hoping to see a lighter from the *Enterprise* come curving down towards him. In that, he had been disappointed. But not really surprised. It wasn't the done thing to leave a bondman in distress—not if you wanted to ensure the loyalty of your staff—but with the partners down on the ground that bastard O'Rourke was in charge, and in his eyes Northrop was a traitor anyway.

His entreaties to Karvass had been unavailing. The Artaxa had looked stonily ahead without answering whenever Northrop tried to explain that he must be taken back to the camp immediately, because of his daily need for water.

Northrop had begun to accept that he was doomed.

He had to admit that the sandboat was a marvellous construction, well adapted to the terrain over which it travelled. Its radium motor humming, it fairly skimmed over the soft yellow sand day and night. In a mostly featureless environment he could not easily estimate its speed, but if he had been told they were covering somewhere between one and two thousand kilometers perplanetary rotation—about thirty hours—he would not have been in the least surprised.

It was yet one more similarity between Tenacity and the fictional Barsoom, he told himself: technical sophistication in a sparsely populated warrior culture (which in the case of the green Barsoomians had been nomadic to boot). In Burroughs' stories that had been a contradiction. It was like expecting Genghis Khan's Mongols to manufacture machine guns.

Yet here, it was a reality.

Then, when the sandboat wound among the hill formation and plunged down the underground bank to emerge into the huge cavern, he almost forgot his plight. Here indeed was a wonder not described in any of the Burroughs Martian books he had read. True, the Tlixix were said to live in domes which might be of comparable size, but they were not like the Barsoomians either. They were more like the hippopotamus-resembling masters of Pellucidar, the world within the Earth. And he doubted if the Tlixix boasted such numbers as he saw jostling on the floor of the great cavern.

Entranced, he gazed up at the mass of glowing crystal of which the roof was composed, turning the whole huge space into an eerie grotto.

Karvass nudged him from the sandboat and towards a line of Artaxa whose skin seemed rougher than his own. Perhaps, Northrop thought, that meant they were older. Their metal ornaments were more numerous, too. His mind went back again to Barsoom, where metal ornaments on otherwise naked bodies were like campaign medals or badges of rank, collected by killing someone.

A younger Artaxa came from somewhere to the side of the welcoming committee. He carried a small bucket-like container with a metal lid, which he offered to Northrop.

Holding it in one arm, Roncie removed the lid. The container held what looked like water, though it was dark and oily-looking.

He was puzzled. The Tlixix were supposed to have all the water on the surface of the planet. He dipped a finger in the liquid and tasted it. It was not salty, at any rate. It tasted like brackish water.

His thirst became overpowering. He lifted the container to his lips and drank, cautiously at first. The water had a strong mineral taste, but it was drinkable.

Gasping with relief, he put the lid back on. Holding on to the container, he turned to Karvass.

"Where did this come from?"

Karvass pointed a lank finger to a group of creatures who were neither Artaxa nor even humanoid. They were vaguely lizard-like, standing erect with a forward-sloping posture, but white as worms which never saw the light.

"Those are our allies the Sawune, who live in deep caverns, much deeper than this. There, they have found water."

So! There was water which the Tlixix had not sequestered, though probably not much. Northrop tried to recall his brief look at the report on the species of Tenacity. Apart from the numerous dehydrate humanoids, there were also dehydrate lizard species, mostly subterranean. It was possible that a few pools of fresh water had survived evaporation in far-down pockets, also escaping detection by the lobsters' enthusiastic water-searches.

A more far-reaching realization came to him, now that the long drink had cleared his mind. His captors had known in advance that he needed water. They had made provision for it.

He turned again to Karvass.

"Thank you. But what about food?"

The Artaxa's facial membranes adopted a configuration. Northrop knew enough by now to interpret this as an expression display, but he didn't know of what. Karvass's verbal response, however, made it clear it was one of surprise.

"But have you not eaten? Surely you do not need to eat again?"

Northrop began to remember some biology. He looked at the compact bodies of the dehydrates. Since they did not have circulating blood, these creatures might not need homeostatic temperature control. It was the high-energy-using warm-blooded creatures that needed to feed every day. A mammal needed ten times as much food as a reptile. The dehydrates, with their bodily process of molecular migration through a gel, would have such fine temperature control, and their bodies would be so economical in the use of its resources, that they probably ate only a few times a year.

That made perfect sense. There would be little enough food to find on this desiccated planet.

So the Artaxa had made no provision to feed their prisoner, beyond grabbing up his breakfast. And whatever they used for food would at best pass right through him, if it did not poison him outright.

He sighed grievously. For all his wandering, this was the first time in his life that he had gone hungry, except by choice.

Hands pushed him towards the elders. Without preamble or greeting, one spoke to him.

"Your kind has been seen in the Pavilion of Audience. You have erected machines in the desert. You have weapons unknown to us. Clearly you are an inventive people. But who are you? By your appearance you are numbered among the races of men, yet water is not poisonous to you and you require it as do the Tlixix. This is a contradiction. Did the Tlixix make you to be their new servants, or are you from some hidden part of the world? Answer, and answer truthfully, unless you wish to test how much torture you can withstand."

Furiously Northrop began wondering what he could say to avoid that threat. Did the Artaxa know any astronomy? Would they understand the idea of a world other than Tenacity?

He set about trying to explain it all. That he and his friends were men, but they came from another world that was full of water, as this one had been when only the Tlixix lived on it. He had expected this to be greeted with incredulity, but not a single facial membrane as much as stirred. The elders simply listened. When he had finished one spoke.

"So you have come to our world from elsewhere, or so you say. And you talk to the masters of our world, the Tlixix. Why? What is your business with them?"

Northrop started thinking hard. *What the hell do I owe Krabbe and Bouche? They wouldn't let me go when I wanted to leave. They locked me up and dragged me out here. Now they've abandoned me to the dehydrates, leaving me to die. Anyway they're acting illegally. Apart from that, their morals stink. These dehydrates will all drown when the ocean comes back. I'm not even sure they can survive on higher ground once the climate changes. But the least they deserve is to be warned.*

He spoke aloud to himself. "All right Karl, all right Boris, here it comes."

He began to spill the beans, again reminding the Artaxa of how Tenacity had once borne a large ocean. In those long-ago days, he said, water had showered from the sky even on to the dry places. They appeared already to know this and became impatient at his words.

But when he told them that those days could be made to return, they were both startled and bewildered.

"This is to happen in the next few days," he said implacably. "All the low-lying areas, including these caverns, will lie under water. If you want to survive you had better move to higher ground."

Not a single one of his listeners stirred or spoke for a long time. Then, in a voice gravid with disbelief, one said, "It is a lie. The creature is trying to panic us into evacuating."

"Put him to the torture," another said.

Yet another spoke up. "Why do you tell us this? It is treason to your kind."

"My masters are acting against the laws of the world we come from,"

Northrop answered. "If they are found out they will be punished. I disagree with what they are doing, but while I was their slave I had to do their bidding. Now you have taken me away from them, I am not their slave."

The most bemetalled of the elders turned to another. "How much eruptionite have we? How many radiators?"

"We have more than a thousand shells of eruptionite," the other answered. "As for radiators, about forty so far."

The chief elder addressed Roncie again. "If your warning is a true one, then you have rendered us a great service. If it is not, your punishment will be a terrible one. We go now to consider your words."

The elders turned as one man and marched into the great crowd thronging the floor of the cavern.

Roncie was left with Karvass, who though badly shaken by everything he had just heard, offered to show him round the underground camp.

"A great enterprise is underway," he revealed. "The tyranny of the Tlixix is over. We and other tribes are ready to rise in revolt. Furthermore we have new weapons and devices which not even the Tlixix have."

In a side cavern he showed Northrop where one of these devices, referred to as 'radiators' was in production. To the Earthman's bemusement it turned out to be a primitive form of radio. Like all early inventions, it was unnecessarily large and cumbersome.

But it followed the general pattern of technology on the desert planet. All powered machinery on Tenacity depended on the presence of the radioactive element radium, plus a means to convert its radioactivity to electric current, which was also due to a serendipitous natural resource. Tenacity was rich in exotic crystals, some of which generated enough electricity to turn an electric motor if placed adjacent to pure radium. Tenacity mechanics had also devised accumulators, again exploiting naturally occurring exotic minerals, able to absorb a hefty amperage at fairly high tension. Hence a radium power source continued to charge up an accumulator whether the machine was in use or not. A Tenacity vehicle could therefore travel at top speed for many days, drawing additional power from a previously charged accumulator.

The layout of the 'radiator' was somewhat similar, except that no accumulator was necessary. Semiconductor crystals sent an oscillating current to the antenna, causing it to transmit a carrier wave which was modulated by means of a simple microphone. In addition there was a speaker for receiving. And that was all. There was no tuning. The frequency was fixed.

Northrop silently saluted the unknown Analane genius—or geniuses—who had discovered radio waves and developed the rig, something which the Tlixix had failed to do throughout their history.

Perhaps, he told himself, Krabbe & Bouche were doing business with the wrong side.

Indeed, no sooner had he finished inspecting the radiator than word came to Karvass. The council had taken his warning seriously. In an effort to avert the catastrophe they were bringing forward the revolt.

Task forces were to set out immediately to launch attacks on the Tlixix hydroriums.

CHAPTER FOURTEEN

The inhabited part of Tenacity consisted of the bed of the dead ocean together with the former shoreline. The old Tlixix civilisation had centred on that shoreline. When the Tlixix created their helper races they confined them to the great empty space around which were ranged the new domes of survival. They had no wish to see those races spread to the highlands, which even before the great dehydration had consisted mostly of desert. They knew they would be unable to exercise control over so vaster an area, and that endangered their security.

Now, from the secret giant camp of the Artaxa, from the camps of the Toureen, from the camps of the Sawune and of those others who had thrown in their lot with the rebellion, which included the Limes and one of the two Jodobrock tribes, motorised war-hordes set out. Gaminte patrols they encountered were wiped out, any individuals who fled or escaped hunted down in the fastest available vehicles. It was essential the Tlixix should not know what was about to hit them.

Had O'Rourke in fact kept a watch to search for Northrop they might have received a warning—supposing anyone had remarked on the number of desert caravans heading for the Tlixix refuges. He had delegated a crew member to make a scan through the interferometric telescope initially, though without moving the *Enterprise* to get a better view. Almost as quickly, he had taken her off the duty to supervise the delivery of shock tubes to the eight sites in preparation.

The Artaxa meanwhile diverted from the main column a detachment to the only one of those sites known to them, and from which Northrop had been taken. They were disappointed to find it abandoned, the tents gone, only the litter of past human occupation remaining. They were not to know that a shock tube had already been put in place and the shaft over it filled in, or that the stiff wire jutting out of the yellow sand was the antenna for the detonation signal.

A hastily set up network of radiators enabled the Artaxa to launch their attacks simultaneously. Carrying flingers specially adapted for throwing spherical shells of eruptionite, the humming columns approached their targets.

When Karl Krabbe felt the first explosion rock the dome of the hydrorium he wondered if Castaneda had jumped the schedule, or worse, something had gone amiss. He got through to O'Rourke on the gogetter ship.

"O'Rourke, what the hell's going on?"

The answering tone was puzzled. "Going on, sir?"

Krabbe formed a suspicion, making him momentarily furious.

"Say, you didn't use any of that prehistoric junk, did you?"

During the early planning Engineering had proposed using an archaic technology—hydrogen fusion—for the shock tubes on grounds of economy. Both Castaneda and Northrop had vetoed that. Hydrogen fusion couldn't be tuned fine enough for a controlled shifting of the tectonic plates without serious risk of widespread vulcanism. The tubes were to use helium fusion, a standard if old-fashioned technique.

"No sir, of course not."

"Well, where's Castaneda?"

"He's here with me now, sir."

Krabbe's fury returned. "Castaneda, what the hell are you doing up there so soon? Why aren't you down on site?"

"I've got lung cancer, sir," Castaneda answered dolefully. "It's all the radon gas I've been breathing, a breakdown product of radium. The atmosphere's full of it. Radpaint can't protect you against that."

"For heaven's sake don't be such a sissy, Carlos," Krabbe said irritably. "Medbay has a spare lung or two, I expect."

While they spoke a barrage of explosions rattled the dome. They were coming nearer. Boris Bouche dashed into the apartment, his face feral with excitement and alarm.

"We're under attack! A revolt against the lobsters! They're using explosives!"

Through the open door Krabbe saw a scene of frenzy. Tlixix scuttled along the passage as fast as their short stick-like legs could take them, roaring ferociously. Black Gamintes also ran, metal accoutrements clinking and clashing.

Krabbe turned back to the communicator. "O'Rourke, we've got a situation down here. What's the status of the project?"

"The last tube has just been put in place," O'Rourke said. "Provisional detonation schedule is, er, right now plus one-seventeen minutes."

"Okay, this is what I want you to do. Pull the team up and detonate *immediately*. Have you got that?"

"Pull up and detonate. Yes, sir. What about yourselves? Shall we come and get you?"

Krabbe hesitated, glancing at his partner. "No, we are still 'honoured guests', so to speak. We're all right for the moment. Keep me informed."

He signed off. "Do you think this attack is serious, Boris? Does it happen often?"

Bouche scowled. "We'd understood the lobsters have everything sewn up tight. And explosives are supposed to be unknown here."

"This is the main hydrorium, for God's sake!" Krabbe found time to smile. "Well, if this *is* a large-scale uprising the lobsters will have double reason to be grateful to us. Detonation is coming. That should put the dehydrates in their place!"

A loud crack and a roar drowned out his last words. There was no doubt that this time it came from inside the dome.

A Gaminte appeared in the doorway.

"Invaders have breached the sacred refuge. You are in danger. Follow me."

Hastily gathering up their effects, the partners hurried after him, away from the fighting.

*

Castaneda himself transmitted the signal that detonated all eight helium fusion devices at the same time. The small planet rang like a bell. The shock was felt everywhere on its surface. A juddering, then another juddering, and another, as seismic waves travelled through the lithosphere and rebounded on themselves, criss-crossing. The first earthquakes for thousands of years shook the desert, knocking down dunes and hills. The underground caves and tunnels of the lizard species crumbled and collapsed, as did most of the caverns of the camp of the Artaxa.

Tlixix engineering proved itself. The ancient cycloidal domes of the hydroriums, large as they were, mostly withstood the shock. Two, however, were weakened and breached by eruptionite. These cracked open like eggshells.

One of them was the largest hydrorium of all.

Such events were incidental and of little importance to those watching and recording aboard the *Enterprise*. They watched with satisfaction as sensors buried in the crust sent back data on tectonic plate movement.

Expectantly, they waited for signs of water.

It was not long in coming. Within the hour damp patches appeared on the surface of the sand. Spectrography detected water vapour in the atmosphere.

Then there came muddy stirrings, followed by gushers, scalding waterspouts leaping high in the air. And then blowers—blasts of steam hissing out of the sand, accompanied by sudden uprisings of the desert floor as vast mounds of hot water forced their way through. An ocean was being squirted up from the planetary aquifer, bringing steamy heat with it. Fog and cloud formed. Soon, it would start to rain.

Already the climate was reverting.

And already the dehydrate tribes were in panic, fleeing the deadly liquid in frantic columns, racing for the high ground beyond the ancient ocean bed. Hrityu, rejoicing in victory over the Crome, watched in disbelief as a surging sand slurry came ripping and flapping at running pace towards the ruins of the Analane camp, before those who could do so piled aboard all available vehicles and departed.

*

The aftershocks continued for several hours. Castaneda gave the partners reports every fifteen minutes. Underneath what Krabbe regarded as his cowardly hypochondria, he sounded quietly pleased. The planet was responding as calculated, the rehydration of Tenacity proceeding according to plan.

Occasionally O'Rourke broke in, asking if the partners needed extracting from the ruined dome. Krabbe declined. He and Bouche wanted to see the ocean coming back first hand, and the Gamintes were now holding their own.

They had been moved to what soon would be the landward side of the dome. But then something even more dramatic happened. Undermined by the rising water table, an entire slab of land collapsed to re-create the wide bay that had existed in former times. It immediately began to fill with boiling, hissing liquid. The broken dome, its foundations undermined, tilted and slid with a grinding sound until partly submerged in the foaming tumult.

In the part that remained above water, fighting continued. With no participation by the Tlixix, however. They abandoned the dome altogether, leaving it to the dehydrates. A frenzy had ripped them. The sight of an emerging sea seized them with an uncontrollable instinct to respond to their evolved nature. Dragging out metal boats stored for millennia somewhere in the dome, they launched themselves on to the heaving, steaming, bubbling water.

The lurch as the dome tilted sent Karl Krabbe and Boris Bouche tumbling against the wall of the cell they now occupied. Luckily, it was in the half of the dome that stayed above water.

Bouche squealed in alarm and pointed upward. The ceiling was bending and collapsing. The cell was being crushed as the dome deformed. The two scrambled on hands and knees from the contracting space and into the corridor. Here, the ceiling was holding. Their Gaminte guard, having regained his feet on the now-sloping floor, was chopping to pieces two green Artaxa, wielding the great curved axe which the Gamintes used for close fighting.

Finishing the work, he gestured to them. "Come, we must escape."

Gladly they followed him through the wreckage of the dome, avoiding the sounds of fighting and the squealings and bangs as the ancient metal structure came apart. Eventually he found a rent where the external skin had ruptured.

They emerged on to what was now a headland. A warm fog was everywhere, a phenomenon which must have seemed utterly strange to the Gaminte. He started coughing continuously and seemed to find it difficult to move. Krabbe wondered what his understanding of the situation was, as he loyally followed orders to protect his charges. Probably he thought the rebel attackers were to blame for everything.

A short distance away lay a large vehicle park, a sort of terminus for traffic to and from the hydrorium. Beckoning to them, the Gaminte went limping towards it.

From not much further off, a red glow could be seen.

The fog cleared a little as they neared the park. The source of the glow became visible, spreading to the edge of visibility. A broad front of hissing, smoking lava was advancing on the dome, already lapping around the parked vehicles.

Castaneda had warned that there would be modest vulcanism in some areas, as increased pressure and temperature on the plate edges caused rock melt to percolate upwards to the surface. He had promised that it would cease once sufficient water had been vented.

Evidently, this was one of the affected areas.

"Karl," Bouche said worriedly, "where's the communicator?"

"Back in the cell," Krabbe said. "I dropped it. Don't worry, O'Rourke will find us."

The Gaminte was heading straight for the lava. He stopped at an odd-looking craft which lacked wheels but stood on bent legs like some huge insect. Attached by struts above the passenger compartment was a large curved structure made of very thin metal. More than anything, it resembled a parachute.

"This one," the Gaminte gasped, still coughing. "Hurry. Mount."

Krabbe held back. "How the hell is that thing going to walk on lava?"

"We'd better do as he says," Boris muttered.

The Gaminte was already clambering aboard. They followed his example, levering themselves over the side.

The coal-black Gaminte, without waiting for them to make themselves comfortable, seated himself at the controls and pulled a lever.

The result was startling. The vehicle leaped high into the air, taking the Earthmen by surprise and sending them tumbling to the floor of the car.

The Gaminte knew what he was doing. He manipulated other levers which altered the angle of the parachute structure over their heads. The vehicle entered a controlled glide.

Peering below them, Krabbe and Bouche could see no end to the lava field glowing through the drifting fog. It was, more correctly, a lava swamp. There were patches of solid ground here and there, the yellow sand seeming to be turning black.

It was towards one of these that the Gaminte was taking them. The machine alighted with the grace of a gull. Its feet seemed to touch the sand for but a moment. The legs bent, bracing themselves, then sprang straight. The leaping parachute machine hurtled froglike back into the air.

"I'll be damned," Krabbe murmured, his eyes dreamy. It was fascinating to see how expertly the dehydrate guided the seemingly clumsy contraption in such difficult circumstances. It was a surprisingly effective way of progressing, if one did not mind the discomfort.

The Gaminte selected a second island in the creeping lava, landed and took off again. He was taking them further from the hydrorium.

But by now he was suffering badly. His coughing increased to a paroxysm, and his hands fell from the controls.

Briefly he seemed to go into convulsions. He fell from his seat. Then he was still.

Krabbe let go an exclamation of shock. "He's died of water poisoning! Boris! We're going into the lava! Do something!"

Cursing savagely, Bouche scrambled into the pilot's seat.

The machine was descending swiftly. He had watched how the Gaminte used the control levers. He experimented, and somehow managed to level out the glide. The machine jolted down. Two legs went into the bubbling melt and two on to sand which immediately crumbled. The vehicle tilted alarmingly.

"Take us up, Boris! We're sinking!"

Bouche yanked on the trigger lever. Again the machine leaped into the air and began its delayed descent. Desperately looking for another landing place, Bouche worked the levers. He thought he was getting the hang of it now. He hit sand, went off again, and now could see the edge of the swamp.

His last landing was most inexpert. The leaping parachute vehicle hit off-balance and toppled over on its side, only yards from the lava flow. They crawled out and looked about them.

A warm wind had sprung up from the direction of the still-forming sea. For a brief spell it swept away the dense fog and they found themselves able to gaze down at the bay where the wrecked hydrorium slumped like a ship that had run aground. The Tlixix, maddened with joy, were trying to sail the boats they had dragged out of the dome.

But they knew nothing about how to manage such craft, which lacked motors and were wind-driven, other than to run sails up the masts. Also, the swirling surface of the bay was unstable. The heat currents that ran through it produced unpredictable boiling areas. As Krabbe and Bouche watched, one of the boats turned over, tipping its crew into the scalding sea. The death hoots of the Tlixix reached the ears of the observing Earthmen.

"*Sweet Krishna!*" breathed Bouche, unconsciously revealing the religion practised by the orphanage where he had been raised. "Just look at it! Boiled lobster!"

Then the fog cut the view off. Krabbe was wondering what to do next when he noticed a shadowy shape moving above the swamp in the murk, heading for the slumped dome. He yelled and waved his arms about over his head. It was a lighter from the *Enterprise*.

Alarmed at the break in communications, O'Rourke had sent a rescue party.

*

Northrop, not having eaten for five days—though he had been given plenty of water—had gone beyond the stage of hunger. But he was feeling weak, and was barely able to stand.

So when the quakes came, he was not at his best. There were countless casualties when the caverns fell in. He had tried to warn the Artaxa that their revolt had come too late.

The shock tubes had been set off. The Great Hydration was beginning.

Perhaps it was his enfeebled state, which the Artaxa were unable to understand, that caused them to ignore his advice. They had been rejoicing when the disaster struck, performing a mass tribal dance. Radio messages had brought thrilling news of the assaults on the hydroriums. Northrop was not taken seriously until those same radio reports began telling of water appearing on the desert floor.

Even then his urgings to evacuate were not heeded. It was when the caves began filling with scalding, steaming water, not his weak voice, that prompted the exodus. Still he was able to explain that they should leave the bed of the old ocean and make for what had been the continental part of Tenacity. He had no idea whether they could survive there, but there was nothing else they could do.

"May all Tlixix die!" Karvass had exclaimed. "No matter if we are to perish as long as we take them with us!"

An understandable sentiment, but Northrop did not see how it could be accomplished.

He was rewarded by being placed in one of the sandboats, whereas thousands of Artaxa and Sawune would have to seek salvation on foot. A lengthy convoy set off for the southern fringe of the old sea bed.

It did not get there. First there came fog, then rain. Finally there appeared an advancing line of sandy sludge.

The convoy could have outrun it for the time being, but by now the dehydrates were dying. The rain was like acid on their naked skin. The fog was like mustard gas in their lungs. The column ground to a halt. The dehydrates, humanoid and lizard, went into convulsions and expired.

Northrop heaved the bodies out of his own vehicle, retrieved a radio rig from another, and continued. But it was not long before the craft bogged down in increasingly damp sand, and would move no further. He would have to walk.

Soon this whole area would be under water. Northrop was making for a clump of hills which would take longer to be submerged, and they were now no more than a kilometer or two away. It was late evening. The usually blazing Tenacity sun created colourful displays on newly formed clouds— which must have been dazzling to any natives still in a mood to behold anything. Cursing the universal tendency for primitive technology always to be too big and too heavy, Northrop dragged the radiator behind him in the sand, now changed from a brilliant sulfur colour to a drab ochre. A canteen of water dangled from his neck. He did not know how he had found the strength to put one foot in front of another, let alone drag the Analane radio too, but the will to survive could work wonders. Not that his prospect of survival was very good.

The sun was still visible when he forced himself up the first hill he came to and set up the radiator. It was simple to operate. He had only to close the switch that completed the circuit to the antenna, and speak into the microphone consisting of a flat plate built into the cabinet.

"Northrop calling the *Enterprise*. Northrop calling the *Enterprise*. I'm in the southern reach of the sea bed. Can you get a fix on me?"

The radiator's ground level range was limited. He was banking on the signal reaching the gogetter ship, no matter how attenuated. Project monitoring included an all-frequency watch—it was one way of detecting what was happening geologically. By now it would be realized that the long-wave, amplitude-modulated analogue signals coming from several sources were artificial. Log procedure would be demodulating and translating those signals.

But would anyone bother to listen to the translations? They had nothing to do with the project. The person on log watch was probably some young girl, the latest recruit to the staff. Would she hear his voice?

It would take a minor miracle.

He carried on speaking into the microphone until his voice was hoarse. Occasionally he switched the apparatus to receive, but all he heard was a faint and distant Artaxa voice bewailing its owners' fate.

The small sun's last rays disappeared. Would it still be freezing cold at night? The cloud cover wasn't thick yet.

He took a last swig from his canteen, then lay down and fell into a stupor.

Maybe dying of exposure wouldn't be the worst thing that could happen.

*

Stepping thankfully into the lighter's cabin, the partners settled themselves into the passenger seats. The door closed. O'Rourke's voice came from orbit.

"Are you all right, Sirs?"

"Yes, we're all right," Krabbe told him impatiently. "Good work, O'Rourke. Might as well bring us up. We'll watch the rest of the show from the ship."

In a flat, casual voice O'Rourke spoke again. "There's been radio traffic on the planet recently, sir. Analogue, amplitude modulated—very primitive stuff. It seems the dehydrate rebels are using it. A few minutes ago the log watch girl heard a voice she recognised. It's Northrop."

He left the last words hanging, as if waiting.

"Got his coordinates?" Krabbe enquired.

"Yes, sir," O'Rourke replied, with a resigned sigh.

"Okay, we'll pick him up on the way, if he hasn't drowned."

He gestured to the pilot. "Move."

The lighter rose into the air. On the view screen, the fog-shrouded scene fell away below.

*

A whistling noise awoke Northrop. Half-frozen, he opened his eyes. His heart leaped when he recognised the outline of the lighter against the stars, hanging over the hillside.

A searchlight shone down. The pilot had spotted him. The lighter came nearer and swung itself level with the hilltop. The door opened to expose a lighted interior.

A sour baritone voice emerged. "Step inside, Roncie."

It was Boris Bouche!

To enter the lighter and find that he had been rescued by the partners themselves gave Roncie an unaccustomed feeling of gratitude—even an unwelcome one. But they ignored his effusive thanks. In fact, they pretty much ignored him altogether. He relaxed in the seat they offered him, enjoying the warmth, experiencing a renewed stirring of hunger, which he took as a healthy sign.

The lighter soared into the blackness of space and sped towards the *Enterprise*. Then, on the approach, the pilot let out an explosive exclamation of startlement.

They all leaned towards the viewscreen. An angular shape was jockeying into position ahead of them.

The partners' jaws dropped.

A Stellar Commission pursuit ship was in the sky.

CHAPTER FIFTEEN

The Investigations Room aboard the pursuit ship *Invicta* was a forbidding place. The walls were panelled in dark brown wainscoting that seemed to press in on the quite small enclosure.

Across a teak table Commissioner Amundsen faced a bleary-eyed Karl Krabbe and Boris Bouche, the latter wearing his typical lopsided smirk. Ranged alongside the pair were planetologist John Spencer (Carlos Castaneda had been Krabbe's first choice, but he was seriously ill and co-matose), lawyer Harold Shelley, Joanita Serstos (though why the partners had included her in their team mystified Northrop), and Roncie Reaul Northrop himself, whose presence had been demanded by the Commission. Krabbe had raised his eyebrows on hearing this, but had made no comment. Northrop guessed, or rather hoped, that it had something to do with his attempted bond renunciation.

He felt much better now that he had fed and rested. Two officials Amundsen had not bothered to introduce flanked the Commissioner on either side, each with a stack of files in front of him. Two armed guards stood against the wall. The *Enterprise*, too, lay under the *Invicta*'s guns. If the gogetter ship tried to depart it would be replaced to junk.

Also, the *Enterprise*'s entire data files had been downloaded into the Stellar Commission ship. The Commission knew everything that had been going on.

Commissioner Amundsen, a purse-lipped man with pale blue eyes, radiated a steely absence of sympathy. His face was like a parchment on which was recorded the worry-lines of a bureaucratic life: battle-scars for which, one suspected, he sought revenge on anyone who crossed his path.

He cleared his throat and spoke dryly. "This is an investigation. It is not yet a trial. Facts will be established. Arguments may be presented. Wherever possible parties involved will be given the opportunity to present evidence."

He touched a key on a small panel before him. On the wall to Northrop's left, wainscoting slid aside.

A large split screen was revealed. They were looking into two other rooms elsewhere aboard the *Invicta*. In one, suitably asperged, were two hoary Tlixix. In the other there squatted two Artaxa.

"The specimens you see will represent the interests on the planet below," the Commissioner went on. "We cannot, of course, arrange for all the species described as dehydrate to be present. The two individuals here were submitted by the tribe most opposed to the species claiming to be rulers of the planet."

Shelley coughed nervously, and spoke.

"Before we proceed, my principals have a right to know how the Commission was apprised of the location of the *Enterprise*. Did this information come from anyone on the staff of Krabbe & Bouche, Partners? I cite Clause Fifteen of the statutes of Bonded Service. An act of disloyalty by a bondperson constitutes a felony. The Commission has a duty to disclose such felony if it has occurred."

Krabbe waved a hand. "Leave it, Shelley. I can't believe any of our people would do that."

Joanita Serstos started in her seat and squealed. She was staring at Northrop.

"So *that's* what you were doing in the communications room!" she declared.

Northrop's heart fell. He looked back at her with feigned incomprehension.

She turned to the partners. "It was just as the survey team was going down. I caught Northrop coming out of the communications shack, where he had no right to be. He could have been sending a message!"

"That's no proof of anything," Krabbe protested mildly, a frown on his big face.

In a stony voice the Commissioner replied to Shelley. "I can confirm that the *Enterprise* transmitted details of its location while in this system, by anonymous voice. Voice analysis keyed out to one Roncie Reaul Northrop, awarded a doctorate in nuclear engineering by the University of Chicago."

Amundsen paused, then added scathingly, "His subsequent career appears to have been undistinguished. Just the sort of drifter to end up with a gogetter firm."

Krabbe looked stunned.

Joanita changed her tack. She looked piteously at Northrop. "Oh, Roncie, why didn't you tell me?" she wailed. "We could have escaped from this dreadful life together!"

She clasped her hands imploringly and appealed to the Commissioner. "Can I talk to you in private, sir? It's Krabbe and Bouche who are the real villains!"

Amundsen responded to the outburst with a patronising smile, his first sign of human feeling. He *harrumphed* and muttered an aside to one of his officials.

"I'll make a note of that."

Thanks a lot, Joanita, Roncie thought. He turned away from the glare of malice which Boris Bouche was directing at the two of them. The woman would obviously do anything to extract herself from an awkward situation, even if it meant betraying her sworn employers.

Amundsen resumed.

"Three indictments have been filed to date. First, the firm registered as Krabbe & Bouche, Partners, has engaged in commercial treaties with alien governments while subject to revocation of licence. Second, the firm registered as Krabbe & Bouche, Partners, has engaged in geological interference of the planet designated Tenacity, to the detriment of its inhabitants, in defiance of Clause Four of the Statute of Alien Treaties. Third, the firm registered as Krabbe & Bouche, Partners, has incurred costs to the state in respect of the state's obligation to remedy such criminal acts."

He paused again to allow this statement to sink in.

Shelley, battling bravely, once more spoke up.

"Commissioner, the firm of Krabbe & Bouche, Partners, strenuously denies all these charges. In the first place, the firm of Krabbe & Bouche, Partners, immediately appealed against the revocation of its licence, and not having been informed of any outcome of such appeal, does not consider the revocation to be in force. Secondly—"

Shelley was following the strategy that any argument is better than none, however flimsy. Amundsen was having none of it. He shot Shelley a threatening glance.

"I have not yet finished."

"Sorry sir," Shelley muttered.

Amundsen went on, "Hereunder are appended the persons answerable for these charges.

"Karl Henry Krabbe, resident upon the star vessel *Enterprise*.

"Boris Oliver Bouche, resident upon the star vessel *Enterprise*.

"Roncie Reaul Northrop, resident upon the star vessel *Enterprise*."

Northrop spluttered. "That's ridiculous! I'm a bondman! I'm not responsible!"

"Normally, that would be correct," Amundsen replied calmly. "A bondperson takes an oath of obedience and so is not accountable for acts ordered by his or her master. However you broke your bond when you informed on your masters to the Commission. You are therefore responsible for your part in the rehydration project, which was a substantial one."

"If it weren't for me you wouldn't be here!" Northrop protested.

Amundsen remained cold. "The law is not to be trifled with. The charge stands." He nodded to Shelley. "Now you may proceed."

Shelley shuffled his papers. "As to the second charge, it has no substance. All my principals have done is to rectify a natural calamity which took place only a hiccup ago in geological time. I cite the precedent of Sauram, Runne and Harker, Partners, who diverted an asteroid on course for Alar IV. I further cite the precedent of Haynam and Khaire, Partners, who rendered assistance to T358 III *after* a comet struck, reverting and stabilising the climate. Neither of these operations was deemed illegal within the meaning of the statute."

Northrop jumped up raving. "Why are you crucifying only me? What about the rest of the staff? *Their* bonds are null and void by reason of revocation of licence! Why aren't all *their* names on the charge sheet?"

"It is a fine legal point, and one which has been amply dealt with by precedent," Amundsen told him implacably, "and not in your favour. "You will resume your seat."

"As for the third charge," Shelley went on after Northrop had subsided in defeat, "it falls down with the second one." He swallowed. "I now request that the Commission allow a submission from the long-term possessors of the planet, who are also signatories to our treaty."

The Tenaciteans had been briefed previously on the form the proceedings would take. An aged Tlixix shuffled closer on the screen. A hoarse but dignified voice came through, rendered into comprehensible speech.

"*What the Earthman says is true. Dehydration is not our world's natural condition. If your laws are just, they will grant us the status quo ante.*"

It fascinated Northrop, despite his predicament, to hear the creature speak in archaic legal phrases. It didn't know any Latin, of course. The translator had simply cottoned on.

The lobsters were proving to be good lawyers.

Not so the Artaxa. One leaped to his feet and seemed about to attack the screen on which the hearing had been displayed. The translator rendered his protests in a reedy, aggressive tone.

"The Tlixix belong to the past! They are but one tribe, and we are many! It is *our* world, and has been waterless since the time of our arising!"

The Tlixix retorted in domineering fashion. "We own you. We created you from lower animals. You have no right to exist at all, except at our behest."

The translator was unable to handle the stream of invective which this statement provoked. It issued a mish-mash of meaningless noise.

"May I say something?" Karl Krabbe asked, with a show of affability. "Frankly, I don't know what this fuss is all about. There's no doubt at all that the lobsters were the political masters of this planet when we arrived, and are biologically superior. You wouldn't do business with somebody's horse or pet dog, would you?"

The second Artaxa jumped up. "But for your interference in flooding the world with an evil fluid, the Tlixix would have been exterminated by now! They do not belong in our world!"

"It is you who will be exterminated," the Tlixix informed him.

"Enough," said Commissioner Amundsen. "I order a twelve hour recess for evaluation of evidence."

He stood up and glared at the partners, with a look which seemed to say, *you have saddled the state with a difficult situation.*

Which was true. If Krabbe & Bouche—and Northrop—were guilty then the administration had a dilemma: either allow the rehydration to persist, with the consequent extermination of all dehydrate tribes, or reverse it, followed by the massacre of the Tlixix. The only way out of the mess was to relocate either the dehydrates or the Tlixix on a more suitable planet, which would be immensely complicated and expensive.

All others in the room followed protocol and rose also. "Fine," Krabbe said, as though the recess had been partly his idea. "May we return to our ship meanwhile?"

Amundsen said crisply. "You will take your rest in the holding cells."

He swept out. Northrop could not help but notice Joanita's fluttering eyelashes, or the Commissioner's attempt to mask his reaction as he left.

*

Despite his continuing tiredness, Northrop did not think he would get any real rest during the adjournment. Lying on a narrow bunk in a metal-lined cell, he tossed and turned, marvelling at the legal tangle in which he had trapped himself.

Yet at some point he must have fallen asleep. He had no idea how long it had lasted when a hand on his shoulder shook him awake.

"Roncie."

It was the thrilling contralto of Joanita Serstos. Northrop forced his drooping eyelids open. Her face hovered over him, misty in his bleary gaze. A glistening grey tab was stuck to her temple. Had she cut herself?

"Get up. Let's go."

The cell door was open. Wonderingly Northrop obeyed. He rose and followed Joanita. A short walk brought them to the Investigations Room. Waiting there were: Krabbe, Bouche, Spencer, Shelley. In other words, the rest of the *Enterprise's* delegation.

Each bore a grey tab on the temple, like Joanita's. Northrop raised a hand and felt his own forehead. He had a tab, too. He tugged at it.

Joanita chuckled. "Don't pull it off, Roncie, or you'll fall asleep again. It won't come off, anyway. I used adhesive."

Northrop's confusion was clearing. He was beginning to understand. He looked straight at the partners.

"Why?"

"We're saving your bacon, Roncie," Krabbe replied dryly. "Let's get out of here."

The party filed through the room's main door, opposite the exit leading to the cells. An alarm began to shrill.

No one seemed perturbed by it. Down the corridor two guards lay sprawled on the floor, snoring.

Led by Boris Bouche, they headed for the skin of the Commission ship, and came to the docking port. A light was on over it, showing that a vehicle was docked on the other side. The inner door was open. O'Rourke stood by it waiting for them. His face betrayed no unusual tension, only his habitual frown of concentration—his badge of determined professionalism.

"Is everything in order, sirs?"

"Everything's fine."

Northrop hung back, wondering whether to run back down the corridor and lose himself in the bowels of the *Invicta*. He was afraid to go with the partners now they knew what he had done. They had the legal right to kill him. He felt lost, trapped, a born loser.

Seeing him about to sidle away, Krabbe glared. "What is it now, Northrop?" he snapped.

"Leave him here if that's what he wants, Karl," Bouche said, a dismissive sneer on his face. "It's what he deserves."

"There's no point in being vindictive, Boris. Or in leaving ourselves short of a top class professional engineer. We've no one to replace Northrop."

"Dummett could do it."

Krabbe shook his head. "He's an amateur. He doesn't have Northrop's qualifications."

He advanced on the quaking Northrop. "All right, Roncie, this is what goes down. You've disgraced yourself, there's absolutely no doubt about that at all. But despite everything, you can still start over. We'll give you a chance to renew your oath to us, if you mean it this time. No jumping ship, no sending sneaky messages behind our backs. But nobody's forcing you. You won't go into the brig, this time.

"If that's not good enough for you, then stay here. And face the Commission's charges all on your own. Believe me, I wouldn't like to be in your shoes if that happens. Amundsen will squash you like a fly."

Northrop blanched. Krabbe pressed home his advantage.

"Tell you what, I'll even throw in Joanita, how's that?"

Just like she was a piece of meat, Northrop thought. Yet he had to admit that the prospect sent a thrill running through him. He couldn't resist glancing at her sidelong. Joanita took him by the hand. "Come on, Roncie, don't be a damned fool."

Limply aware that in truth this was the only way out of the legal trap he had set himself, he allowed her to lead him through the port. The eight of them made the lighter's cabin crowded. O'Rourke handled the controls. He disengaged from the port and ferried them the short distance to the *Enterprise*. Behind them, the *Invicta* lay dead in space, effectively unmanned.

Minutes later they had gathered in what was generally known as the Ops Room. Joanita was applying a freezing cold liquid to the grey patches, enabling her to peel them off. Boris Bouche rubbed the frigid sensation from his temple with his fingers. He glanced accusingly at Northrop.

"Take a lesson from this, Roncie. Some people still know how to serve their masters. Miss Serstos has behaved magnificently."

"Yes, I think I've worked out why she was included on the defence team," Northrop replied, in his best sarcastic voice. He added, "I take it you've used a neural damping field."

"Obviously. But first we had to switch off the *Invicta*'s electronic defences. That was Joanita's job."

Pulling a tab off Shelley, Joanita smiled with pleasure at the praise she was receiving. "Three hours in the Commissioner's private quarters! That old stick is sure going to be mad when he wakes up."

Krabbe too had a broad smile on his face. "Bureaucrats are such fools! All she had to do was flutter her eyelashes and Amundsen was practically giving her the keys to the kingdom!"

You had to hand it to the partners, Northrop thought. They really knew how to exploit people's talents.

A neural damper was not a common device, but as a pursuit ship the *Invicta* would be protected against that and similar perils by a buffer field. The partners' answer was simple. Get Joanita to disable the buffer.

The grey tabs were an antidote. They stimulated the brain's mechanism for consciousness arousal, the ascending reticular system, and so kept one awake even inside a damping field. Joanita would have been wearing one when she turned the buffer off. O'Rourke, watching like a spider on the *Enterprise*, would have seen the buffer go down and projected the damper in almost the same instant. With everyone around her unconscious, all Joanita had to do then was find her way to the cells and apply tabs to the partners and their bondmen.

A most resourceful woman. An asset to the firm of Krabbe & Bouche, Partners.

Northrop wondered briefly if he had unwittingly played a part in the theatrical performance at the hearing. Had his defection already become known?

No, he didn't think so. Krabbe's shock had been genuine.

"A neural damper," he repeated. "That's illegal technology."

He had not seen it or the reticular stimulator before, though he had heard the latter could be a mind-bending torture instrument, keeping a victim awake indefinitely. Bouche answered with a dirty chuckle.

"Sure it is. But I'm not certain we actually used it. At least, I doubt if Amundsen will put it in his report. He'll be too embarrassed."

"Let's go," Krabbe ordered.

The drive was engaged. The *Enterprise* shot off into interstellar space, to look for pastures new.

CHAPTER SIXTEEN

Holding the traditional oak rod in his right hand, for the second time in his life Roncie Reaul Northrop intoned the words that put him in fealty to Karl Henry Krabbe and Boris Oliver Bouche, Partners. They held similar oak rods. They promised to protect him and to treat him well. Remuneration was not mentioned. By custom that resulted from some vague notion of 'reciprocal good will' that was supposed to arise between master and bondperson.

Northrop knew what was coming next. The short ceremony over, its record safely locked in the ship's files (alongside the first identical ceremony) it was customary for the master to give his new slave a moral homily. This one would not be like the first. Karl Krabbe put on the pained and anxious expression Northrop had seen so many times when he was about to give someone a dressing-down.

"You do understand, Roncie, that this time it's real? This time you can't go through the form then change your mind like you did before. Conduct like that is bad for you, bad for us, bad for everybody. Now I'm going to be straight with you. I know you resented it when we stopped you leaving us. I suppose you imagine we were thinking only of ourselves, but that's not true! After all, we can always get another nuke man. No, we had your welfare in mind just as much, if not more so, as ours. We take our oaths seriously, even when you don't. We're *responsible* for you, you're like *family*. Let's face it, where were you when we recruited you? In a bar, half drunk, with no money and no prospects. A drifter and a bum. You may be a fine engineer, but when it comes to taking charge of your own life you're hopeless. Without us to take care of you, you'll never amount to anything."

Northrop felt uncomfortable. Krabbe and Bouche were adept at the avuncular act. But he didn't like to admit that there was something to what Krabbe had said. He liked to think of himself as an individual.

Then why had the partners' offer seemed such a haven, that first time?

Krabbe was finishing his speech. "So whatever criticisms you have of us, I want you to voice them now."

He said this with an air of fairness rather than confrontation.

Northrop ground his teeth.

"I don't like people who are prepared to extinguish entire races for the sake of profit!" he blurted out.

Krabbe blinked, as if taken aback.

"Maybe you just don't understand business."

Boris Bouche, who up to now had sat by saying nothing, stirred and intervened. "If you have such high and mighty ideals, Roncie, why did you cooperate with the rehydration project? You could have sat in the brig and refused to have anything to do with it."

"I was under bond," Northrop muttered.

"So what? If it meant that much to you, you could have refused orders and taken the consequences."

"I did do something," Northrop said defensively. "I sent a warning to the Stellar Commission. I had hoped they would stop the project before any harm was done."

"Did you? I looked at the communications log. It has no record of your transmission. The log can't be falsified. The only way it doesn't register a call is if you fail to contact the destination before sending. You transmitted blind rather than risk discovery, didn't you? Your message had maybe a five per cent chance of being received."

Bouche licked his lips, a wolf getting ready to pounce. "Your character is weak, Northrop, as Partner Krabbe says. It's neither one thing nor the other, neither good nor bad. You're incapable of making decisions and sticking to them. You need the discipline of the firm to give you strength of purpose. While you're with us you have the opportunity to develop and strengthen your personal qualities. In fact, we insist on it. Remember that this is a two-way relationship. We can renounce the bond too. If you disappoint us again, we may have to do that. In which case I have no doubt you will end up as a derelict."

Northrop was silent. Better not to disclose how he had tried to sabotage the project a second time by warning the dehydrates. That had not really influenced events, anyway.

"I did accomplish something. The Commission will have to sort matters out, accommodating both sides, though I suppose in the end that will mean giving either the lobsters or the dehydrates a new world and moving them there."

Bouche propped his head on his hand, his lopsided smile becoming almost sad. "You really think so? Governments are very ethical, of course. They always do the right thing. The harm wrought by those wicked gogetters has to be put right! Let me explain how it will be done. Shelley has looked at the legalities of it. He thinks they point to the lobsters keeping a watered Tenacity and the dehydrates being relocated to another desert planet. That's a very expensive option. The decision is too big to be made *in situ*, aboard the *Invicta*. It will have to be made by some committee back home. Also the project will have to be costed and funded, and that's a Treasury matter. So the issue gets batted back and forth for a while. Eventually, as a first step, the Treasury releases funds for a fact-finding mission. It rushes to Tenacity, only to report that it's too bad, nothing can be done, the dehydrates are extinct. No further funds are required.

"See how it works? Delay is the bureaucrat's best friend. Anyway half the dehydrates are dead already even as we speak. Who cares? They are an artificial lifeform which would never have evolved by itself. The lobsters made them for a specific purpose, and that purpose is over. So you see, Roncie, your little act of treason, feeble as it was, didn't alter a thing. We've done our job. We've given the lobsters what they wanted, and we've got their signatures on the contract. There'll be a good return on it eventually, and there's a share for you too."

There was a slight shifting sensation as the *Enterprise* changed course yet again, seeking to shake off the *Invicta*'s pursuit that would now be taking place.

Northrop's heart sank. The pursuit had little or no chance of tracking them down, and it would not persist for long.

But every day it lasted lessened the dehydrates' already slender chances of survival. His mind filled with images of the brave desert warriors, struggling to beat the odds stacked against them.

Boris Bouche was pure cynic. He assumed that everyone was as unprincipled as himself, including the Stellar Commission and all other arms of government. But for the sake of the green men of Tenacity, the blue men, the black men, the men of every colour on the small planet, fighting and striving with all the courage and intelligence they could muster, he hoped that Bouche, for once, was wrong.

www.ingramcontent.com/pod-product-compliance
Lightning Source LLC
Chambersburg PA
CBHW020700180626
46816CB00003B/1375